Samuel French Acting Edition

New York Stories

Five Plays About Life in New York

by Jason Milligan

I0589018

‖SAMUEL FRENCH‖

SAMUELFRENCH.COM **SAMUELFRENCH.CO.UK**

ISBN 978-0-573-62359-2

www.SamuelFrench.com
www.SamuelFrench.co.uk

FOR PRODUCTION ENQUIRIES

UNITED STATES AND CANADA
Info@SamuelFrench.com
1-866-598-8449

UNITED KINGDOM AND EUROPE
Plays@SamuelFrench.co.uk
020-7255-4302

Each title is subject to availability from Samuel French, depending upon
country of performance. Please be aware that *NEW YORK STORIES* may
not be licensed by Samuel French in your territory. Professional and
amateur producers should contact the nearest Samuel French office or
licensing partner to verify availability.

social media websites.

For all enquiries regarding motion picture, television, and other media rights, please contact Samuel French.

MUSIC USE NOTE

Licensees are solely responsible for obtaining formal written permission from copyright owners to use copyrighted music in the performance of this play and are strongly cautioned to do so. If no such permission is obtained by the licensee, then the licensee must use only original music that the licensee owns and controls. Licensees are solely responsible and liable for all music clearances and shall indemnify the copyright owners of the play(s) and their licensing agent, Samuel French, against any costs, expenses, losses and liabilities arising from the use of music by licensees. Please contact the appropriate music licensing authority in your territory for the rights to any incidental music.

IMPORTANT BILLING AND CREDIT REQUIREMENTS

If you have obtained performance rights to this title, please refer to your licensing agreement for important billing and credit requirements.

For Stefanie . . .

TABLE OF CONTENTS

FOREWORD

All of the plays included in this volume have been produced in New York, each as a separate entity in various evenings of original one-act plays.

Knowing that each piece stands on its own, I selected these specific plays to go together so that, if desired, they could be played collectively as an evening of theatre. The theme: Life, in and around this bizarre place we call New York City.

Yes, one takes place in New Jersey. And another in Queens. And yet another in Brooklyn. But they're all part of that same scary, funny, frightening world that we New Yorkers share and which I have enjoyed sharing with theatregoers.

Provided in the back of this collection is a cast breakdown, in the event that you would like to produce this group of plays as an evening. The minimum casting requirement for all five plays is 4 men and 3 women.

SHOES

Shoes was first produced at Actors Theatre of Louisville on May 29,1984, under the direction of Robert Spera. The cast was as follows:

JIM .... Michael Lubeck
TONY .... John Zarchen
FOREIGNER .... Mark Fredo

The set was designed by Sandra Strawn; costumes were by Katherine Bonner; lighting was by Geoff Korf; and the Production Stage Manager was Chip Washabaugh.

Shoes was subsequently produced at the Noel Coward Theatre in New York on August 8th, 1984 under the direction of Fred Sanders, as part of an evening called *Outlines*. The cast was as follows:

JIM .... David Spera
TONY .... John Zarchen
FOREIGNER .... Kevin Cristaldi

The lights were designed by Craig Weindling and the Production Stage Manager was James M. Bay.

CHARACTERS

JIM, the diner owner.

TONY, his brother.

A FOREIGNER.

SETTING

A small diner. Downtown. Six a.m. on a Monday morning in the present. The dead of winter.

SHOES

AT RISE: JIM is behind a counter doing various restaurant-related tasks (polishing silverware, sweeping, wiping down the counter, and so on). HE wears weathered work pants, a once-white dress shirt, and a spattered white apron. His brother TONY sits on the other side of the counter, reading a newspaper. TONY is dressed in one of those double-knit suits that comes with a reversible vest and two pairs of pants.

TONY. *(As HE reads.)* Jesus Christ! Three more inches.

JIM What?

TONY. They're predicting three more inches of snow. God, I can't believe it.

JIM. Great. Business isn't bad enough already, Mother Nature's gotta shit on me too.

TONY. That's good, Jim. That's good. I tell ya, you're really a poet. Ya know that? *(Laughs, goes back to paper.)* Hey! They got the money.

JIM. What?

TONY. The money. They finally got the money. Thank God.

JIM. What the hell you talkin' about?

TONY. The city got the rest of its funding on the, uh … for renovating Downtown here. You hear about that?

JIM. Yeah.

TONY. About time. Maybe now they'll do something about it. No offense, but this whole neighborhood looks like shit. Comin' down today, I see the street's still all torn up outside.

JIM. Yeah.

TONY. (*Referring to the article.*) I think that's great. People finally takin' some action, y'know? You oughta read this.

JIM. What?

TONY. This article. It's really good. You oughta read it.

JIM. When do I have time to read? I don't sit on my ass in one o' them foam-padded swivel chairs all day long like SOME people.

TONY. So? Take a break.

JIM. A break?

TONY. Yeah. I mean, jeez, you been runnin' around in here since, what, five-thirty?

JIM. Five.

TONY. Five. Jeez, see what I mean? Siddown a minute.

JIM. I can't siddown, Tony. I gotta lotta stuff to get done here.

TONY. Whatever you say, Jimbo. YOU'RE the boss. (*TONY laughs at his remark. Pause. TONY starts drumming on the counter.*) Where's my coffee?

JIM. Hold onto your ass a minute. There's more perking, it ain't ready yet.

TONY. What, does it take all day?

JIM. Maybe it does. Trouble with you always was you was too damn anxious.

TONY. You sound like Dad.

JIM. Don't start that.

TONY. Sorry. (*Silence for a moment.*) What time is it?

JIM. What?

TONY. The time. What time is it?

JIM. Is my last name Timex?

TONY. No.

JIM. Then what the hell you askin' me for? You gotta watch.

TONY. I know. But it's more fun raggin' you about it. (*Pause.*) My eggs ready yet?

JIM. Your what?

TONY. My eggs.

JIM. What do you think?

TONY. I dunno.

JIM. Watch me carefully. WHAT DO YOU THINK?

TONY. I think, probably not.

JIM. You think right.

TONY. Well could you hurry 'em up or somethin'?

JIM. You want 'em so bad, YOU go cook 'em.

TONY. Jeez, some brother you are. I'm starvin' here. What, you gonna let me die of starvation?

JIM. Hey, you die in here it ain't gonna be from starvation.

TONY. What then? Ptomaine?

JIM. More like this broom 'gainst your head! (*Calling to kitchen.*) HURRY UP WITH THE SCRAMBLED EGGS!

TONY. Poached.

JIM. What?

TONY. Poached. I told you I wanted them poached.

(*A FOREIGN MAN enters and stands near the exit, shyly. HE wears a suit and tie that is fashionable in his own country but he has no shoes or socks on. He is unnoticed by JIM and TONY.*)

JIM. Poached? Who the hell eats eggs poached?

TONY. I do, all right?

JIM. Well today you'll eat 'em scrambled.

TONY. C'mon, Jim—

JIM. Look, if all I had to worry about was how my eggs was fixed, I would be a happy man!

TONY. Boy, are you on the rag today. Where the hell is Donna? She always gets it right.

JIM. I had to let her go.

TONY. How come?

JIM. I just did.

TONY. 'At's a shame. Nice girl. God, what a great ass. (*Pause.*) So, you the only one here?

JIM. What does it look like?

TONY. Hey, I'm just askin'.

JIM. Yeah. I'm the only one here. 'Cept Chuck.

TONY. The cook.

JIM. Yeah. Damn rush starts at six-thirty, how the hell am I gonna handle it alone?

TONY. You always do.

JIM. What do you mean?

TONY. You always say you can't handle it—even with Donna here—but you always do. It's like some kinda tradition with you, like—

JIM. Like what? You and poached eggs on Monday mornings?

TONY. Yeah, I guess so.

JIM. (*To Foreigner.*) You want somethin'? (*No answer.*) Hey, you!

(*The FOREIGNER looks at Jim, but no answer.*)

JIM. What, you gonna stand there all day, or you want somethin'?

(Again, no answer.)

TONY. Maybe he's deaf. Do some sign language.
JIM. Sign la—what, am I a social worker?
TONY. Hey, I'm just kiddin'.
FOREIGNER. *(Timidly.)* Please?
JIM. Huh?
FOREIGNER. PLEASE?
JIM. What?
FOREIGNER. Is being very lost much. Most needs be directions.

(Silence a moment. Then, JIM and TONY burst out laughing.)

TONY. This guy is great. Maybe we could get him on *David Letterman.*
JIM. I dunno, he sounds like he's on dope or somethin'. *(To Foreigner.)* Hey. Hey! What're you talkin' about?
FOREIGNER. Am for to be ... boos. Boos? *(Trying to say "bus.")* To take me for to ... understand not for to be ... boos, take me to for be ... which can for.

(The FOREIGNER believes he has made perfect sense. HE waits for a reply. Silence for a moment.)

TONY. What's this guy talkin' about?

JIM. I dunno, but I don't have time for this. I gotta fix the coffee and clear the register, and—

(JIM has started moving towards the Foreigner. The FOREIGNER pulls a folded-up piece of paper from his pocket and hands it to him. A moment of silence as JIM reads. The FOREIGNER looks on hopefully. In a moment, JIM begins to laugh.)

TONY. What's it say? Jokes?

JIM. No, lissen to this: *(Reads.)* "Please, can you show me to the subway?" "Where can I find the bathroom?" "Which way is the exit?"

(TONY and JIM have found each expression progressively funnier. The FOREIGNER, thinking that communication has been made, smiles and nods his head vigorously.)

JIM. *(To Foreigner.)* Oh, you wanna see the exit? There's the exit. "Please for to use exit." *(JIM shoves the Foreigner out the door.)*—and get your ass outta here! *(To Tony, as HE returns to his spot behind counter.)* This is just some cute scam of his to make money. It ain't gonna work on me.

(The FOREIGNER has re-entered, unnoticed by JIM.)

FOREIGNER. *(Blurting out, in desperation.)* Please to be for help me!

JIM. *(Moving towards Foreigner.)* This guy don't take no for an answer!

TONY. Wait, this guy is foreign or somethin'. You speak any foreign languages?

JIM. What, am I a college professor?

TONY. I'm just askin'. Maybe he's lost. Maybe he doesn't know where he is. Maybe—

JIM. No "maybe's" about it. He's a bum. (*Giving list to Foreigner.*) Go on. Take a hike.

FOREIGNER. (*Puts the paper back in his pocket and takes out a bus ticket.*) Please. Boos for to take port.

TONY. What, is that a bus ticket he's got there?

JIM. I dunno. (*To Foreigner.*) You can't eat on bus tokens. (*No answer.*) We don't take SUBWAY TOKENS!

TONY. I think this guy is really lost or somethin'. Ask him. Ask him if he's lost.

JIM. Don't give me this shit—

TONY. Just ask him, okay? Ask him if he's lost. C'mon.

(*Pause. Then, JIM reluctantly addresses the Foreigner.*)

JIM. Are you lost? (*No answer.*) Are ... you ... lost?

FOREIGNER. Loost? Boos for to be boos loost?

JIM. Ya see this? We are wastin' our time with this guy. He's a stinkin' bum, I told you that—

TONY. No, he's not a bum. I mean, look at that suit. That's a nice suit.

JIM Oh, very attractive. Get serious! He doesn't even have any shoes on. Look. No SHOES!

FOREIGNER. Shoes!

JIM. What?

FOREIGNER. Shoes! Please for tell where for have to have shoes!

JIM. C'mon, buddy. Let's go.

(JIM reaches for the Foreigner's arm, but TONY stops him.)

TONY. Wait, I think he WANTS a pair of shoes.

JIM. Oh, sure he wants some shoes. Maybe he'd like a new car too?

TONY. No, I'm serious. I think he WANTS some shoes. I mean, he doesn't have any on.

FOREIGNER. Shoes. For to be wanting shoes.

JIM. So? What am I supposed to do about it? I don't owe him anything. *(Advancing on Foreigner.)* I'm not gonna tell you again. Now beat it!

TONY. *(Steps in between Jim and the Foreigner. To Jim.)* Wait, lemme talk to him.

JIM. What are you doin'?

TONY. Don't worry about me. Go back to work.

JIM. Look—

TONY. Go on back to work. You said you had so much to do, go do it. I wanna talk to this guy.

(Pause. JIM reluctantly returns to counter.)

TONY. *(To Foreigner.)* Ahem. Uh … Good Morning. Where… uh, where do you come from?

FOREIGNER. SHOES!

JIM. Shit, this guy is gettin' on my nerves.

TONY. I'm takin' care of this. *(To Foreigner.)* Okay. Mr. Shoe.

FOREIGNER. Shoes?

TONY. Yeah. Shoes.

FOREIGNER. Shoes.

TONY. Uh-huh.

FOREIGNER. Shoes.

JIM. Oh, you're makin' major breakthroughs here.

TONY. I'm not done yet, willya shuttup?

JIM. Excuse me. (*JIM busies himself behind the counter.*)

FOREIGNER. Shoes. Where for to buy shoes?

TONY. Wait, you wanna BUY shoes?

FOREIGNER. (*Nodding.*) Shoes!

TONY. (*Triumphant, to Jim.*) HEY! He wants to BUY shoes!

JIM. That's what it looks like.

TONY. Send him to the shoe store.

JIM. The what?

TONY. The—the shoe store! Tell him how to get to the shoe store!

FOREIGNER. Shoe store?

TONY. Yeah! They sell shoes!

FOREIGNER. Shoes! Yes. Shoes! Want for to buy SHOES!

TONY. That's it! THAT'S IT! He wants to buy shoes! See that bus ticket? He wants to GO to a shoe store!

FOREIGNER. Shoes! Shoe Store! Buy Shoes! Shoe Store!

JIM. (*Topping them both.*) Wait a minute! WAIT A MINUTE! (*Silence.*) There ain't no shoe stores open at six a.m., hot shot.

TONY. Shit, you're right.

FOREIGNER. (*Senses the disappointment of the other two.*) Shoe store?

TONY. No. Shoe store closed.

FOREIGNER. Close?

TONY. Shoe store ... not yet to for be open.

FOREIGNER. Heh?

JIM. That's right. Confuse him.

TONY. Well, what're we gonna do?

JIM. Throw him out.

TONY. You can't Just throw him out. It's cold out there. He ain't got no shoes on. Or haven't you noticed?

JIM. My heart bleeds for the bastard.

TONY. No, really. We can't Just throw him out in the street like yesterday's garbage.

JIM. Sure we can.

TONY. But he could die or somethin'. He looks kinda sick. Like he hasn't eaten in awhile.

JIM. So what d'you want ME to do? Feed him?

TONY. Why not?

JIM. This ain't the Red Cross.

FOREIGNER. Shoes. Nowhere stay to. Please ... cold ... warm me help me for to.

TONY. Sounds like he ain't got nowhere to go.

JIM. I dunno.

TONY. Don't you care?

JIM. Look, it ain't our problem. Somebody'll help him. If he needs help.

TONY. He looks really hungry. My eggs. Let him have my eggs.

JIM. No way. I ain't servin' him in here. Can't you read that sign on the door? "No Shirt, No SHOES, No Service."

TONY. We have to help this guy.

JIM. "We?" What's all this "we" shit?

TONY. You're supposed to help people in need—

JIM. Since when? Huh? Some people don't wanna be helped. Some people wanna be left alone.

TONY. You think this guy WANTS to be left alone? I mean, what the hell are you talkin' about?

JIM. Never mind. Just never mind. I ain't got time for this shit. This place is gonna be packed in fifteen minutes.

TONY. So?

JIM. So I don't want him in here.

TONY. That's pretty selfish, you know that?

JIM. Why me? I don't see YOU bendin' over ass-backwards to help him out.

TONY. Who the hell's been talkin' to him for the last ten minutes?

JIM. All you ARE is talk. You wanna help him so bad, go ahead. Take him home with you. Get him drunk. Let him sleep in your bed—

TONY. Look, I don't wanna be his drinkin' buddy, I want you to feed him. This is a diner; give him the goddamn eggs!

JIM. No, this is MY diner. You don't tell me what to do.

TONY. Well, evidently SOMEbody has to. You're not doin' so well by yourself.

JIM. Get out of here.

TONY. No.

JIM. Get the fuck out of here!

TONY. I'm not leavin'.

JIM. Fuck you!

TONY. Fuck YOU!

FOREIGNER. Shoes!

JIM. (*To Foreigner*.) SHUTTUP!

FOREIGNER. Shoes! For to be wa—

(At this point, JIM may either shove the Foreigner violently or throw something at him.)

JIM. SHUTTUP! JUST SHUTTUP YOU FUCKING RAG-HEAD! *(To Tony.)* And YOU. I'm not gonna say it again. You get the hell out of here and take him with you.

TONY. What IS it with you today?

JIM. I am SICK of people wanting to HELP other people. I'm SICK of hearing you go on and on about it. "I got a great idea, Jim, let's join Save the Whales"; "I gotta great idea, Jim, let's send money to feed the Starving Children in India"; "Look, Jimbo! Isn't that great? They're renovating DOWNTOWN! That's great, Jimbo, isn't it? ISN'T THAT GREAT?" Well, buddy, do you think it's "great" that I have to sell-out and LEAVE this place for them to renovate downtown? Oh, you didn't know that, big fella, did you? Well, here it is. I got this yesterday. *(JIM produces a letter and hands it to Tony.)* They told me I have to up-and-leave MY diner. So. They renovate. Kick me out. Where the hell am I gonna go? I ain't got nothin'. But you don't have to worry about that. You've never had to worry about ANYTHING. You've always been away at college or sittin' in your nice little office. And you think comin' by here once a week makes up for it all? Well it don't. It sure as hell don't. So you go on. Talk all you want about helping people. But I am sick of hearing it. Who's helping me, huh? WHO IS HELPING ME?

(Silence. For a long while.)

FOREIGNER. *(Softly.)* Shoes ... cold—

*(TONY puts his finger to his lips to say "be quiet." The
     FOREIGNER repeats the gesture. The FOREIGNER
     understands. It is quiet for quite some time. Then,
     TONY slowly approaches Jim.)*

TONY. If you'll give him my eggs, I'll take him and
buy him some shoes. And then I'll get him on the bus and
try to help him get where he's goin'. And then ... I'll
come back here. Take the day off. And I'll ... come back
here.

*(Silence as the TWO BROTHERS communicate for the
     first time in a long while. THEY may or may not look
     at each other. But there is a silent reconciliation of
     differences. And then JIM exits to get the eggs.)*

FOREIGNER. *(Quietly now.)* Shoes. Please ... for to
help me ...
     TONY. It's okay. Here. *(Covering FOREIGNER with
his own coat.)* We're gonna get you some shoes.
Everything'll be all right. Just put this on so you stay
warm.
     FOREIGNER. Shoes?

*(The FOREIGNER sits and lays his head down, TONY
     helping him.)*

FOREIGNER. Shoes. *(FOREIGNER's words grow
softer as the LIGHTS begin a slow fade.)* Shoes.

TONY. It's gonna be all right. We'll get you your shoes. And you'll have shoes just like everybody else. Soon.

FOREIGNER. (*Falling asleep.*) Shoes.

BLACKOUT

THE BEST WARM BEER IN
BROOKLYN

The Best Warm Beer in Brooklyn was originally presented at Ensemble Studio Theatre as a work-in-progress in April, 1986, under the direction of the author. The cast was as follows:

JOEY ....Angelo Tiffe

EDDIE ....Kevin Cristaldi

THE BIG TEXAN ....Charles Lynch

The Best Warm Beer in Brooklyn was presented in its first full production at the West Bank Cafe Downstairs Theatre Bar in New York on February 14, 1989 with the following cast:

JOEY ....Donald Kimmel

EDDIE .... Edward Patrick Corbett

THE BIG TEXAN .... Steven Griffith

The production was directed by Steve Rankin; lighting design was by Josh Jenkins.

CHARACTERS

JOEY SPANO, the bar owner. Big athletic-looking Italian fellow. Mid-thirties.

EDDIE, the writer. Unshaven, unkempt. Frayed. Driven by a "vision."

THE BIG TEXAN. He is pissed. Justice to him is his rifle, which he carries in a gun rack in his El Camino. Along with the spurs that hang from his rear-view mirror.

SETTING

The action takes place at JOEY's bar in Brooklyn.

Three o'clock in the morning.

The present.

THE BEST WARM BEER IN BROOKLYN

SETTING: Brooklyn. JOEY SPANO's bar. Three o'clock in the morning.

AT RISE: JOEY, a mid-thirties athletic-looking Italian guy is closing-up the place: washing glasses out, wiping the counter, etc. It's obviously hot as hell—a huge floor fan on a stand blows a breeze on Joey from across the bar. A bright yellow industrial extension cord leads across the stage to the fan. JOEY crosses to the fan, stands in front of it, lets it cool him a bit. EDDIE enters. HE is unshaven, unkempt, wears dirty old clothes, looks like a bum. JOEY does not see Eddie. EDDIE stops, stares at Joey, speaks.

EDDIE. You open?
JOEY. (*Turns to face him. Beat.*) Depends. Whatcha want?

(*Beat.*)

EDDIE. (*Looks around.*) Beer.
JOEY. What kind?
EDDIE. Bud.
JOEY. Bottle?
EDDIE. Yeah.
JOEY. Well ... drink it fast. I'm closin'.

(JOEY serves Eddie a bottled Bud. JOEY resumes cleaning up. EDDIE stares at him.)

JOEY. What?
EDDIE. Huh?
JOEY. What're you starin' at?
EDDIE. Nothin'.
JOEY. C'mon, drink up, okay? I gotta get outta here.
EDDIE. You're—ah—
JOEY. What?
EDDIE. This is your place, right?
JOEY. Yeah, it's my place, will you drink your beer?

(EDDIE kicks over a stool.)

JOEY. Hey. You drunk, mister?

(No answer. JOEY eyes Eddie warily for a moment, then returns to his work. EDDIE stands on the counter.)

JOEY. What're you—hey! Get offa there!

(EDDIE does not.)

JOEY. You hear me? *(No answer.)* C'mon buddy. It's three o'clock in the morning! I wanna close up and go home, okay? I ain't got time for this shit.

(EDDIE does not come down.)

JOEY. Look, come on down or I'm gonna BRING your ass down, ya hear me? *(No response.)* Hey. I do you a favor: I let you come in for a fuckin' beer, now you do me a favor and drink the damn thing and GO, okay?

(Pause. EDDIE kills it.)

JOEY. Good. You was about to piss me off there.

(EDDIE spits a mouthful back at Joey.)

JOEY. SON-OF-A-BITCH!

(JOEY grabs Eddie and violently brings him down. THEY knock over stools; JOEY throws Eddie over a table and is about to punch his lights out when HE suddenly stops and stares at Eddie. Pause.)

JOEY. Hey. Do I know you?
EDDIE. *(Great urgency.)* Go ahead! You were about to hit me—!
JOEY. *(Trying to remember.)* I know you from somewhere ...
EDDIE. Don't stop now!
JOEY. Who are you?
EDDIE. Just hit me!
JOEY. WHO THE HELL ARE YOU?
EDDIE. HIT ME, JOEY!

(Beat; JOEY pulls back.)

JOEY. How do you know my name—? *(Beat.)* Huh? *(No answer.)* WHO THE FUCK ARE YOU?
EDDIE. EDDIE!

(*JOEY just stares.*)

EDDIE. EDDIE LEFKOWITZ!

(*Pause.*)

JOEY. (*Thinking.*) Eddie Lefkowitz ... Eddie ... Lefkowitz. Shit, yeah, I remember you! Eddie Lefkowitz! I ain't seen you since fuckin' high school!

EDDIE. I know!

JOEY. You look fuckin' awful.

EDDIE. I know. I been sufferin'.

JOEY. Sufferin'?

EDDIE. Yeah.

JOEY. Hey, I'm sorry about your nose, fella.

EDDIE. S'okay.

JOEY. It's bleedin'.

EDDIE. That's great. I mean, I'm fine—it's okay.

JOEY. Here, you better sit down, pal. You wanna go wash your face in the men's room or somethin'? I got some dishwashin' stuff you can use for soap.

EDDIE. No, I'm okay.

JOEY. Y'sure?

EDDIE. Yeah.

JOEY. Y'want another Bud?

EDDIE. Yeah, sure.

JOEY. Comin' up. (*Crosses to bar.*) Man if you aren't still weird as hell. You always were weird as hell.

EDDIE. Yeah, well—

JOEY. I always wondered what the fuck happened to you. You was the only one, moved away. Everybody else stayed.

EDDIE. Everybody?

JOEY. Yeah. Ted and Ernie, they opened a ribs place out in Astoria. Carla Patka, she married some rich casino-hotel guy, gives her a black eye every once and awhile. Old Wally Lewis, he died. Old Strongman?

EDDIE. Strongman died?

JOEY. Yeah. Me and him was wrestlin' champions back in high school, 'member?

EDDIE. And he's DEAD?

JOEY. Yeah. Heart attack. Can you believe it? Thirty years old and he dies of a fuckin' heart attack.

EDDIE. How? He was always so healthy.

JOEY. Yeah, but he was always LIFTIN' things. Chairs, cars, pianos. Showin' off them muscles. One day he tries to lift a dumpster, a goddamn dumpster, he just turns real red and keels over. I seen it. Bright red. And then—klunk. Dead.

EDDIE. God.

JOEY. Yeah. (*Beat.*) I was a pall-bearer.

EDDIE. Huh. (*Pause.*) So how you been?

JOEY. Ah, well, stable. I guess that describes me best. Everything's stable.

EDDIE. Good.

JOEY. Put a little money away, you know. Nutshell.

EDDIE. That's good.

JOEY. Yeah. I had this place, eight years now. Same people, y'know. Stable.

EDDIE. Yeah. Stable.

JOEY. Beer nuts?

EDDIE. Sure.

JOEY. So what you been doin' with your life, Eddie? 'Sides spittin' out beer?

EDDIE. I'm a writer.

JOEY. Writer?

EDDIE. Yeah.

JOEY. Writin' books?

EDDIE. Novels, yeah.

JOEY. Novels.

EDDIE. Yeah.

JOEY. I always figured you'd do somethin' brainy like that. You was the smartest guy in school. I mean, we were all fuckin' stupid, but you was the smartest outta alla us. You used to do my homework for me.

EDDIE. You made me. You used to beat me up if I didn't.

JOEY. Yeah. But I appreciated it though.

EDDIE. Yeah.

JOEY. So what's the name a your book? Maybe I seen it in the B. Dalton's window.

EDDIE. No.

JOEY. Maybe.

EDDIE. No you didn't. Cause it never got PUBLISHED.

JOEY. Oh. Was it not any good?

EDDIE. It was GREAT! I worked my ass off on it. I spent two years writing the damn thing, Joey. I sent it to seventy-six different publishers. Seventy-six! And do you know what all of 'em told me?

JOEY. What?

EDDIE. That I wasn't WORDLY ENOUGH to write a book. Some said that I was "too young" and had not had "enough experience to sustain a novel." Some a the others told me I hadn't "suffered enough."

JOEY. Well I don't know about that—

EDDIE. Believe me Joey, when seventy-six different people tell you you haven't suffered enough, you begin to BELIEVE you haven't suffered enough!

JOEY. I guess you're right.

EDDIE. Damn right I'm right.

JOEY. Lemme show you something. (*JOEY takes out his wallet, digs through it.*)

EDDIE. What?

JOEY. (*Holding a woman's photo up.*) My wife.

EDDIE. Wow. She's beautiful.

JOEY. Yeah. Name's Rosa. Idn't she just fuckin' magnificent?

EDDIE. Yeah. Lemme see …

JOEY. (*Almost hands it over, stops.*) Are your hands clean?

EDDIE. Sorta.

JOEY. Well, be careful. Don't dirty her up.

EDDIE. (*Gazing at the photo.*) I had a wife.

JOEY. Yeah?

EDDIE. Yeah. (*Puts the photo in his shirt pocket.*)

JOEY. (*Leaping up.*) HEY! That's my wife you just put in your pocket!

EDDIE. I know.

JOEY. Give her back!

EDDIE. I'll give her back, don't worry.

JOEY. Give her back NOW!

EDDIE. I'll give her back in a minute—

JOEY. NOW!

EDDIE. IN A MINUTE!

JOEY. NOW, GODDAMMIT!!

EDDIE. HIT ME!

JOEY. (*Stunned.*) What?

EDDIE. HIT ME! Hard as you can!

JOEY. Jesus Christ, what is it with all this violence shit anyway? Are you, like, cracked-up in the head?

EDDIE. No! Hit me!

JOEY. No.

EDDIE. I won't give her back till you hit me.

JOEY. Well I'm not gonna hit you, ya damn fool. I'm twice your size, I'd probably cripple you for life!

EDDIE. I KNOW!

(Pause.)

JOEY. I got other pictures anyway.

(EDDIE looks at Joey's wallet, which is lying on the table. JOEY grabs it, puts it away.)

EDDIE. Well, I don't got any pictures a mine. She took 'em all. She took EVERYTHING! Left me with nothin' but my dirty underwear and a Pulsar watch!

JOEY. That's bad.

EDDIE. I know.

JOEY. Well, you don't seem too sad about it.

EDDIE. I'm not! I'm GLAD she did it! I WANTED her to do it!

JOEY. Why the hell would you want THAT?

EDDIE. See, I wanted a woman with expensive tastes who was beautiful that I could fall madly in love with but never hold on to. A marriage that was doomed to fail.

JOEY. Yeah, but why would you WANT that?

EDDIE. I figured that would definitely lead to some serious sufferin'.

JOEY. Yeah, but WHY would you want that?

EDDIE. So I could write my BOOK!

JOEY. Oh. (*Beat.*) So what happened?

EDDIE. It worked!

JOEY. Yeah?

EDDIE. Yeah! I lusted after her; she got sick a me. I convinced her I was rich: I took out a huge loan, I couldn't pay it back—she got stuck with that—she divorced me, sued the hell outta me, took everything I had, even took my KID!

JOEY. Kid?

EDDIE. Yeah. We had a girl. Sally. She's five now.

JOEY. You got a picture a her?

EDDIE. No. My wife took it.

JOEY. Aw, sorry.

EDDIE. No, no, don't feel sorry for me! I WANTED it to happen! I WANTED to suffer so I could become a great writer! Only the artist who suffers creates lasting art! All those guys in the old days who cut off their ears and all? All that great shit! I wanted to be like *them*!

JOEY. So ... did it work?

EDDIE. No.

JOEY. Oh shit.

EDDIE. Yeah. See, I rewrote the book after my divorce and I sent it out to the same seventy-six places.

JOEY. And what happened?

EDDIE. I got the SAME seventy-six replies!

JOEY. Shit!

EDDIE. Yeah. So I thought about it and thought about it and I decided, y'know, maybe I hadn't suffered ENOUGH.

JOEY. I see that.

EDDIE. Yeah. So I thought, y'know, crime and jail and prison and all that shit would be pretty rough.

JOEY. Oh, sure.

EDDIE. Yeah. So I figured if I could get sent to prison I could get gang-raped or somethin', you know, really suffer!

JOEY. That would be sufferin', yeah.

EDDIE. I know!

JOEY. So what'd you do?

EDDIE. I robbed this Lotto stand!

JOEY. Yeah?

EDDIE. Yeah! Got away with five thousand dollars! And they CAUGHT me too!

JOEY. Great!

EDDIE. Yeah! And I went to court and my wife came in as a character witness, tore me to RIBBONS!

JOEY. ALL RIGHT!

EDDIE. YEAH!

JOEY. SO DID YOU GO TO PRISON?

EDDIE. No. I goofed, see.

JOEY. How?

EDDIE. I told 'em WHY I did it, you know, cause I wanted to suffer so I could write my book?

JOEY. Yeah?

EDDIE. And they figured I was *crazy* and so they put me in this MENTAL PLACE!

JOEY. Aw, shit.

EDDIE. Yeah. But that was pretty bad.

JOEY. Yeah?

EDDIE. Yeah. People eatin' crayons and shit. Peein' in their pants. It was pretty awful.

JOEY. So then you suffered there?

EDDIE. Oh, yeah. Boy did I.

JOEY. Wow.

EDDIE. Yeah. So. I got outta there a year and a half ago. And I plunged myself right back into my work; I rewrote the book and sent it out again.

JOEY. The same seventy-six places?

EDDIE. Yep. The same seventy-six. And guess what?

JOEY. The same letter?

EDDIE. No. This time I got a DIFFERENT letter …

(EDDIE, of course, has it unfolded by this time and holds it out for Joey to see. JOEY reads.)

JOEY. "Dear Mr. Lefkotz—"

EDDIE. They always spell it wrong.

JOEY. Oh. "We were pleased to read your new ms—"

EDDIE. That means manuscript.

JOEY. Oh. I knew.

EDDIE. Oh. Okay.

JOEY. "… we are pleased to say it is much improved, but still does not reflect a well-rounded experience with life. Thanks for sending it in. We always enjoy new works." Huh. All of 'em said that?

EDDIE. Most of 'em, yeah.

JOEY. Oh.

EDDIE. Yeah. *(Pause.)* So all I need, I think, is a little more suffering.

JOEY. I would guess so, yeah.

EDDIE. (*In one breath.*) I mean, I lost a wife, a kid, my house, my car, almost my sanity, my right to vote or hold office; I'm a criminal and a deadbeat and I ain't got NOTHIN'! YOU'D THINK I COULD WRITE A GREAT FUCKIN' BOOK!

JOEY. I know!

EDDIE. (*The master plan here.*) But ya see? It's so simple: only one thing is missin'.

JOEY. Yeah?

EDDIE. Yeah. It was starin' me in the face all the time.

JOEY. What?

EDDIE. Broken bones.

JOEY. Broken bones?

EDDIE. Yeah. maimed, hurt, in pain—me! That's all I need! Then I KNOW I can sit down and write the Greatest American Novel full of life's experiences and woes!

JOEY. Yeah.

EDDIE. Yeah.

JOEY. (*Uneasily.*) Uh ... yeah.

EDDIE. Yeah.

(*Pause.*)

JOEY. So ... what is it you want ME to do? Hit ya or somethin'?

EDDIE. That was my initial idea, see. But I got a better one ... (*Drops a set of car keys on the table.*) I stole this car today. El Camino. I want to stand out there in the street and you to run over me.

JOEY. RUN OVER YOU?

EDDIE. Yeah! Idn't that GREAT?

JOEY. Jesus, I can't do that!

EDDIE. Why not? Christ, I don't want you to KILL me, just break a few bones, coupla ribs—

JOEY. No.

EDDIE. Please.

JOEY. Never. No. You're fuckin' crazy!

EDDIE. I'll dedicate the book to you!

JOEY. NO!

EDDIE. Please, Joey, you GOTTA!

JOEY. Why ME?

EDDIE. You used to beat me up all the TIME in high school, you never ONCE hurt me REAL bad!

JOEY. That was high school!

EDDIE. But I need somebody I can TRUST! I could just go jump off a roof or stick my head in that fan over there or somethin' but I want to keep my torment within *reason* here! See, I can TRUST you Joey!

JOEY. Don't trust me—!

EDDIE. Joey, you're the toughest guy I ever knew! If ANYBODY could do it without flinchin', it's you. Just mess me up real bad and then you can go back to bein' stable. I won't never bother you again, I swear. Please!

JOEY. It's not—I can't go back to bein' stable!

EDDIE. What do you—what the hell you talkin' about?

JOEY. It can't be stable no more. It's all—(*Beat.*)— look, I got an idea, Eddie. You say this is a stolen car, right?

EDDIE. Yeah.

JOEY. How 'bout we both get in it and I drive it off a bridge and we BOTH die!

EDDIE. Shit, I don't wanna DIE!

JOEY. Well I DO!!!! (*JOEY breaks into sobs.*)

EDDIE. Jesus Christ, whasamatter, Joey?

JOEY. Stable, shit. Ain't nothin' stable. Ten years and it's all over. You call that stable?

EDDIE. What?

JOEY. She left me, Eddie! I loved her with all my heart and she left me. She was a latent lesbian all these years, left me for a goddamn Go-Go Dancer!

EDDIE. God Almighty. I'd never a known.

JOEY. I know.

EDDIE. You're so ... together.

JOEY. Stable, right?

EDDIE. Yeah. Stable.

JOEY. I tell everybody I'm stable, but down inside, in my soul, Eddie, it's eatin' away at me!

EDDIE. What is?

JOEY. "IT," Eddie, "IT!" You gotta know what "it" is, Eddie, you been talkin' about sufferin' all night!

EDDIE. Well ... I guess my "it" is a little different from your "it"—

JOEY. You gotta help me, Eddie! Nobody knows, I'm tellin' you! Nobody in the whole wide fuckin' world! Nobody but you!!!

(JOEY throws himself into Eddie's arms or collapses on the table. EDDIE stands there for a moment, not knowing quite what to do here.)

EDDIE. Hey. So you lost your wife, Joey. Big deal. I lost mine. I kept goin'. You gotta keep goin'. It's not the end a the world, you lose a wife. Coulda been worse! Coulda lost your whole business!

JOEY. I AM gonna lose my business.

EDDIE. What?

JOEY. I got rent due, I can't pay it. I got no money. I'm three weeks overdue, any DAY now they're gonna kick my ass OUTTA here—

EDDIE. Joey—

JOEY. I BEEN SLEEPIN' on this COT in the back room, Eddie! Business has been so fuckin' bad I can't keep my APARTMENT—!

EDDIE. Joey, wait a minute—

JOEY. THIS IS ALL I GOT LEFT EDDIE! (*Pulls out money.*) Eighty-Five Dollars! MY FUCKIN' LIFE SAVINGS!

EDDIE. I thought you said you had a nutshell.

JOEY. Uh—well, I did.

EDDIE. Where is it?

JOEY. I—I can't tell you.

EDDIE. C'mon, Joey. Tell me.

JOEY. No. I can't. I'm too embarrassed.

EDDIE. Joey—

JOEY. You don't know! Nobody could know! She wouldn't love me! She COULDN'T love me! I was desperate, doncha see? I woulda given *anything* to have her back! My LIFE even!

EDDIE. Whoa, Joey, what does this hafta do with the nutshell?

JOEY. Nutshell?

EDDIE. Yeah.

JOEY. What nutshell?

EDDIE. Your nutshell. Your money.

JOEY. My money.

EDDIE. Yes.

JOEY. I spent my money.

EDDIE. I know that already. On WHAT?

JOEY. What?

EDDIE. What did you spend it on?

JOEY. I'm not tellin' you.

EDDIE. Joey—

JOEY. I'm not.

EDDIE. Come on.

JOEY. No.

EDDIE. Please.

JOEY. No.

EDDIE. For 'Ol Eddie.

JOEY. You'll laugh.

EDDIE. I won't.

JOEY. You will.

EDDIE. I won't, I swear.

JOEY. You swear?

EDDIE. Yeah.

JOEY. On your mother's grave?

EDDIE. She ain't dead yet.

JOEY. Then swear on her life.

EDDIE. What?

JOEY. Swear on your mother's life.

EDDIE. Joey, Just tell me—

JOEY. On her life! You swear to me on your mother's life that you won't laugh.

EDDIE. I won't.

JOEY. 'Cause if you laugh, your mother drops dead. Klunk. Like Strongman.

EDDIE. I will NOT laugh. (*Pause.*) I swear. On my mother's life. (*Pause.*) So what did you spend the money on?

(*Pause.*)

JOEY. A sex-change operation.

(Pause. EDDIE bursts out laughing.)

JOEY. YOUR MOTHER JUST DIED, YOU LOUSY LYING SON OF A BITCH!

EDDIE. You?

JOEY. Shut up!

EDDIE. YOU had a sex-change operation?

JOEY. Get outta here!

EDDIE. YOU did?

JOEY. Get the fuck outta here!

EDDIE. No, tell me.

JOEY. No, I didn't have one, you little shit.

EDDIE. You just said you did.

JOEY. No I didn't, I said I put the money down on one.

EDDIE. What?

JOEY. I had to put the money down. As a down payment. I gave it to this clinic out in Rockaway?

EDDIE. Yeah?

JOEY. The next week I take the R train out there for this "counseling session," they call it …

EDDIE. Yeah?

JOEY. And they ain't THERE no more!

EDDIE. No shit?

JOEY. Naw. Fuckin' fly-by-night sons of bitches. Took my whole life savings and flew. Five thousand dollars. I hope they fuckin die! I hope all their hair falls out from syphilis or their kids are born blind. Or SOMETHIN'! Jesus, how could they do that to a guy?

Take all his money and then not give him a sex change?
That sucks, Eddie. That really sucks.

EDDIE. Well, did Rosa know you was havin' a sex-
change operation?

JOEY. No. I was gonna surprise her.

EDDIE. It woulda surprised her all right. What if she
didn't WANT you as a woman? Then you'd a been stuck.
You might not a made such a hot woman anyway, y'know.
You got real hairy arms—

JOEY. DON'T SAY THAT! God, she's ALL I GOT
TO LIVE FOR!!!! (*JOEY breaks into sobs again. Pause.*)

EDDIE. You know where she is?

JOEY. No. Somewhere in South Dakota.

EDDIE. You got an address?

JOEY. No. Just this. (*Pulls out a matchbook, shows it
to Eddie.*) All I got left a her. She used to work there. The
Pussycat Club in Glad Valley, South Dakota. Got it from
one a her woman friends. Natasha.

EDDIE. (*Studying it.*) Huh ...

JOEY. Shit, Eddie, if I had that money back, I'd use it
all to find her. I'd just leave this place and go.

EDDIE. As a man?

JOEY. As a man. If it took weeks or months, or even
YEARS, I wouldn't care. I don't even know how big
South Dakota is, but I'd comb every square inch of it until
I found her. Then she'd see how much I love her. And she'd
have no choice but to come home. To me. (*Pause.*) God, I
need a beer.

EDDIE. How 'bout a hot one?

JOEY. HOT ONE? What do you want with a hot beer?
It's burnin' up in here!

EDDIE. I told ya. I want every bit of agony I can stand.

JOEY. Well ... I'm pretty sick of agony ... but there's some warm ones over there under the counter.

EDDIE. (*Gets them.*) Here ya go. (*A toast.*) To discomfort.

(THEY drink.)

JOEY. Ooh, that's ... that's discomfort.

EDDIE. God, Joey, I gotta admit, I ENVY you. You sound like you were really caught in the throes of anguish. Lots more so than me.

JOEY. Don't envy me, Eddie. It ain't been a shitload a fun.

(As THEY drink, THEY can and should make sour faces at the taste of the unrefrigerated beer.)

EDDIE. Hey, Joey. Listen. There's gotta be answers to both our problems. And if we use our heads, there might maybe possibly be a way to solve two birds with one rock.

JOEY. Rock?

EDDIE. Yeah. Now let's think about this now. You need money, right? So you can go find Rosa.

JOEY. Right.

EDDIE. And I need to get maimed. Right?

JOEY. Right.

EDDIE. So the question is, how is there a way that we can accomplish both things at the same time?

JOEY. I dunno.

(Silence for at least fifteen seconds. THEY think.)

JOEY. Any ideas yet?
EDDIE. No, not yet.

(Pause. THEY think some more.)

JOEY. We better think a somethin' soon. I gotta clean up here in a minute.
EDDIE. *(Beat. An idea dawns on EDDIE.)* Hey.
JOEY. What?
EDDIE. Maybe that's it.
JOEY. What?
EDDIE. Cleanin' up.
JOEY. What?
EDDIE. When you clean this place up at night, what do you use?
JOEY. Rag.
EDDIE. No, ON the rag. What do you PUT on the RAG?
JOEY. Cleaner.
EDDIE. Show me.
JOEY. *(Hands it over to Eddie.)* Here.

(EDDIE holds it triumphantly in the air.)

JOEY. So?

(EDDIE pours the cleaning fluid all over the floor.)

JOEY. What are you DOIN'?
EDDIE. If this place was to, like, burn, would you get insurance money?
JOEY. Sure. I got two policies.

EDDIE. Okay. If I was to get burned, like, real bad, would I suffer?

JOEY. Oh shit yeah. I suffer when I stay out at Jones Beach too long.

EDDIE. Then give me a match. And all our problems are solved.

JOEY. What, are you serious?

EDDIE. Yep. Gimme a match.

JOEY. I ain't got a match.

EDDIE. You gotta have a match. This is a bar.

JOEY. So?

EDDIE. So: bars always got matches.

JOEY. Not mine.

EDDIE. Jesus, ONE MATCH!

JOEY. I ran out!

EDDIE. You got to be kiddin'!

JOEY. I'm serious!

EDDIE. So where the hell are we gonna get some matches.

JOEY. Store.

EDDIE. Any stores around here?

JOEY. Sure.

EDDIE. Great.

JOEY. But it's three in the morning. None of 'em are open at three in the morning.

EDDIE. Shit!

JOEY. Look, this is a stupid idea anyway.

EDDIE. Why?

JOEY. Well, if you burn the place down—well I—I won't have a place.

EDDIE. But you'll have the money.

JOEY. Well, yeah … but—

EDDIE. They will GIVE you the money to fix up the bar. But you don't have to fix up the bar. You can take the money and go.

JOEY. Go find Rosa?

EDDIE. Sure.

JOEY. What about you?

EDDIE. You're gonna save me.

JOEY. Save you?

EDDIE. Yeah.

JOEY. How?

EDDIE. Just stand over there in the corner. And when I look like I've had enough, just grab me and get me out.

JOEY. Stand over there?

EDDIE. Yeah.

JOEY. In the corner?

EDDIE. Yeah.

JOEY. But ... it's gonna be on fire, right?

EDDIE. Right.

JOEY. What if I get burned?

EDDIE. Be careful then.

JOEY. I will, but still. Shit. I might get burned.

EDDIE. But you're a tough guy, Joey. C'mon, all I want is a few messy burns, is that a lot to ask of an old friend?

JOEY. But I HATE burns! I fell asleep out at Jones Beach that time, I was out in the sun SIX HOURS; I was a fuckin' mess!

EDDIE. This ain't sunburn, Joey. It's different.

JOEY. It's still burns.

EDDIE. Joey—

JOEY. Eddie, shit! Burns are the only thing in the WORLD I'm scared of—

EDDIE. Don't be scared—

JOEY. But I am! I'm no pussy, you know that. Hoods don't scare me; Guns and knives don't scare me; but BURNS! Shit, Eddie—don't you WONDER why I got no fuckin' matches in here? Jesus, shit, it's my LIFE PHOBIA!!!

(Dead silence.)

EDDIE. God or somebody does not want me to write this book.

JOEY. I'm sorry, Eddie. I'm—sorry.

EDDIE. Don't be sorry.

JOEY. Well I am.

EDDIE. Well don't be.

JOEY. Well I am.

EDDIE. Shut up, okay? 'Cause I got an idea. *(EDDIE has unplugged the fan, starts coiling the yellow extension cord.)*

JOEY. Hey, what are you doin'? I'm burnin' up in here!

EDDIE. It's gonna be a helluva lot hotter in a minute. *(EDDIE wraps the cord around his hand and yanks it to test its tautness. HE tosses it out to its full length to see how long it is.)*

EDDIE. Perfect!

JOEY. What are you gonna do? Hang yourself?

EDDIE. What?

JOEY. Yeah. Hey, now that's a good idea. You hang yourself off this beam here—it'll hold you—and you can leave everything to me in your will.

EDDIE. I ain't got no will.

JOEY. Here. Write one on this coaster. Leave everything to me and I can go find Rosa and still have my bar.

EDDIE. But I'll be dead.

JOEY. Huh?

EDDIE. You keep forgettin' Joey. I don't wanna DIE. Just be miserable.

JOEY. Oh.

EDDIE. Yeah. So here's what we're gonna do. I'm gonna tie this cord to this chair here. And I'm gonna sit in the chair in the middle a the room.

JOEY. What about me?

EDDIE. You're gonna be outside.

JOEY. Good.

EDDIE. And so I'll set this place on fire. And I'll sit down, see? Like this. And when I've had enough, I'll start screaming. And you pull me out.

JOEY. What if it doesn't work?

EDDIE. It'll work.

JOEY. You sure?

EDDIE. Sure. Just remember to pull fast. I don't want real BAD burns.

JOEY. All right.

EDDIE. Nothing too serious. Just a few third-degrees on my arms and legs.

JOEY. Okay.

EDDIE. Okay.

JOEY. There's only one problem.

EDDIE. What?

JOEY. We still don't have no matches.

EDDIE. (*With a fiendish grin.*) Oh yes we do.

(Pause.)

JOEY. NO!

EDDIE. Joey—

JOEY. I ain't givin' 'em to you!

EDDIE. Why not?

JOEY. 'Cause.

EDDIE. 'Cause what?

JOEY. They're all I got LEFT a her!!

EDDIE. Then just give me one.

JOEY. No!

EDDIE. ONE MATCH!

JOEY. NO! It's my ONLY CLUE to findin' her! If I lose it, I'm fucked!

EDDIE. I'll give it right back!

JOEY. You will?

EDDIE. I will. I promise.

JOEY. Yeah, you promised you wouldn't *laugh* either—!

EDDIE. That was different. Now come on, give 'em here—

JOEY. How?

EDDIE. What?

JOEY. How was it different?

EDDIE. It just was!

JOEY. No it wasn't!

EDDIE. Yes it was! Now come on!

JOEY. And you promised you'd give her PICTURE back, you didn't do THAT either!

EDDIE. Here then, take it—

JOEY. No, you've SWEATED all over it now—

EDDIE. Just give me a match!

JOEY. No!

EDDIE. You want ROSA, don't you?

JOEY. HELL YEAH!

EDDIE. THEN GIVE 'EM HERE!!! (*JOEY still will not.*) It's the only chance you got of gettin' her back, Joey. It's a foolproof plan.

JOEY. Bullshit. You been tellin' me all YOUR foolproof plans all night, NONE of 'em worked—

EDDIE. Joey, just GIVE 'em to me!

JOEY. No!

EDDIE. If you don't give 'em to me, you'll NEVER see Rosa again! (*Beat; EDDIE lets this one sink in.*) They'll kick you out in the street and you'll turn into one a those homeless people. And one day, Rosa will bump into you at Madison Square Garden or some place and she'll say, "Ooh, yuck! What a dirty, scummy CREEP!"

JOEY. She wouldn't say THAT.

EDDIE. (*Forboding.*) Are you SURE?

(*Pause; JOEY cannot hand them over fast enough.*)

EDDIE. Okay. Good. (*EDDIE pulls back the cover. There is one left.*) Jesus, one left! This must be an omen.

JOEY. I guess so.

EDDIE. Okay. So … (*HE is about to light it; stops.*) I'm nervous.

JOEY. Yeah.

EDDIE. Hey. A toast first. For good luck?

JOEY. Yeah. Good luck.

EDDIE. (*Raising his glass.*) To our new lives.

JOEY. (*Raising his too.*) New lives.

EDDIE. And the best warm beer in Brooklyn!

JOEY. Yeah!

(THEY kill the beers.)

JOEY. Whew!
EDDIE. Okay.

(EDDIE strikes the match. HE smiles. JOEY returns the smile nervously. EDDIE crosses over the where the cleaner has been poured; slowly, carefully. JOEY follows. EDDIE is almost there when JOEY suddenly blows the match out. THEY both freeze for a moment. Dead silence.)

EDDIE. *(Very quietly.)* You blew it out.
JOEY. Eddie …
EDDIE. YOU BLEW IT OUT!
JOEY. I'm sorry, I
EDDIE. Why did you blow it out, huh?
JOEY. I dunno, I—
EDDIE. Answer me Joey, WHY! WHY IN GOD'S GIVEN NAME DID YOU BLOW THIS THE FUCK OUT?
JOEY. I don't know!
EDDIE. Why?
JOEY: I don't KNOW, okay?
EDDIE. I was ALMOST THERE!
JOEY. I got scared!
EDDIE. Well, shit, Joey, we're BOTH scared!
JOEY. You're not scared of fire!
EDDIE. What IS it with you and all this FIRE shit, Joey?

JOEY. Nothin—
EDDIE. Joey—
JOEY. Leave me alone!
EDDIE. Tell me JOEY—!
JOEY. SMOKEY THE BEAR!

(Beat.)

EDDIE. What?
JOEY. I—Smokey the Bear came floodin' into my head, Eddie, I felt guilty—
EDDIE. Jesus Christ, Joey, you killed our only fuckin' chance in the world because of a make-believe BEAR?
JOEY. I couldn't HELP it! When I was a kid, I used ta have these nightmares about him comin' ta get me! And you lit that match—and his big, furry face just came flashin' into my HEAD—Shit, I can't explain it Eddie!
EDDIE. Great! That's just GREAT! Nothin' short of a fuckin' *miracle* can save us now!

(Suddenly and without warning, the door to the bar is kicked open. THE BIG TEXAN stands there, LIGHT pouring in from behind him. The effect should be similar to that of the angels appearing before the shepherds. Only this angel wears boots, jeans, a down vest, long underwear shirt, and carries a rifle. Perhaps HE has a saddle slung over his shoulder. JOEY and EDDIE stare at him open-mouthed for a long time in silence. Then:)

TEX. 'At's mah fuckin' car outside. (*Pause*.) Which one a you sons a bitches stole mah fuckin' car? (*Pause*.) If you don't tell me, I'll just shoot botha ya.

JOEY. He did.

TEX. (*Crossing to Eddie*.) Why you little son of a bitch, steal mah car right out from under me while I'm watchin' the goddamn Super Bowl.

EDDIE. Super Bowl?

TEX. Yeah. And you better be glad the Cowboys won too, or I might be in a bad fuckin' mood. And I hate ta think what I'd do ta you if I was in a bad fuckin' mood.

JOEY. Super Bowl?

TEX. That's what I said, ain't it?

JOEY. In July?

TEX. I got a collection, dipshit! A videotape collection of all the games the Cowboys ever played.

EDDIE. I didn't know there were cowboys in New York. I wondered why there were spurs hangin' from the rear-view mirror.

TEX. (*Pointing the gun*.) HEY! You better watch that smart mouth a yers, boy!

EDDIE. Sorry.

TEX. Shit. There I was. Halftime. Super Bowl VII. Mah Favorite. Dallas was kickin' them Miami asses 21-7. So I go runnin' outside ta buy some more beer nuts for the second half ... and my goddamn El Camino is gone!

JOEY. I got beer nuts. You want beer nuts?

TEX. Shuttup, you. (*To Eddie*.) I been walkin' all over Brooklyn since seven o'clock now, boy. Gimme my goddamn keys.

EDDIE. Here.

TEX. Good. Now come on.

EDDIE. Uh ... where?

TEX. For a ride, asshole. You're goin' fer a little ride with me.

EDDIE. You ... you're not gonna ... kill me, are you?

TEX. Hell no. But I'm gonna teach you a lesson you ain't gonna forgit.

EDDIE. Oh—?

TEX. Yeah. Now let's go, boy.

EDDIE. Bye Joey. Thanks for everything.

JOEY. Uh, yeah. Can ... can I help you Eddie?

TEX. You stay right where you are, or I'll plug you in the face.

JOEY. I'll just stay here.

EDDIE. Joey ... I hope everything works out for you.

JOEY. (*Not too hopefully.*) Yeah.

TEX. (*To Eddie.*) Move your ass, geek.

EDDIE. Can I ask you somethin' first?

TEX. What?

EDDIE. You got a match?

TEX. What, you take mah car, now you want my fuckin' matches too?

EDDIE. Not for me. For him. Please.

(*TEX looks over at JOEY, who gives him a very benign smile. TEX grumbles and pulls a book of matches out of his jeans pocket and hands them to Eddie. EDDIE crosses to Joey and hands them to him.*)

EDDIE. Here. (*Takes Rosa's photo from his pocket, hands it back.*) Now you FIND her ...

JOEY. Thanks Eddie.

(A bittersweet smile is exchanged between them.)

TEX. Okay now. Let's go.

EDDIE. *(To Tex.)* You're not gonna, like, break my RIBS or anything are you? How 'bout just my TOES? I mean, that'd still hurt like hell and you'd get the satisfaction outta harming me and, well, you know, I don't NEED to walk all that much anyway—

TEX. Will you shut the hell up and just *go*? I'm gonna DO whatever I damn well *please!* Pushy little twerp!

(Beat.)

EDDIE. *(To Joey.)* I see a best-seller in my recent future.

(EDDIE crosses to door, TEX follows, gun on Eddie. THEY exit. JOEY sits alone in silence for a moment. Picks up the matches, looks at them. Chickens out, puts them down. Takes a sip of the warm beer. Beat. HE picks up the matches again, stares at them. Makes a decision. HE pulls back the cover and strikes a match.)

BLACKOUT

NEXT TUESDAY

Next Tuesday was originally produced in New York by Silver Lining Productions at the Sanford Meisner Theatre on April 20, 1988 under the direction of the author. The cast was as follows:

MICKEY .... Edward Patrick Corbett

BESS................................Stefanie Milligan

The Production Stage Manager was Linda Key; Lights were designed by Josh Jenkins; Sound Design by Jim Bay; and Costumes were designed by Andrea Tilton.

CHARACTERS

MICKEY, a jailbird. Late 20s, early 30s.

BESS, a church counsellor. A year or two younger.

SETTING

The action of the play takes place in the waiting room of a Queens County prison. The time of the play is Spring, 1955.

Scene 1: A Tuesday afternoon.
Scene 2: Tuesday afternoon, a week later.
Scene 3: Tuesday afternoon, two weeks later.
Scene 4: Tuesday afternoon, four weeks later.
Scene 5: Tuesday afternoon, four weeks later.

NEXT TUESDAY

AT RISE: Prison waiting room. MICKEY stands on one side of the stage, BESS is seated on the other. There is one of those visitors' tables stage center with a wire screen in the middle; this separates the two halves of the stage. BESS sits, waiting. MICKEY paces in his area, continually looking up at Bess' side but not seeing who he's looking for. BESS looks up at him; looks down at her lap. Looks up at him again. BESS clears her throat and speaks.

BESS. Ahem ... Mr. Stiletto?

(Beat. HE stops, looks at her.)

MICKEY. ME?
BESS. Ex—excuse me?
MICKEY. You talkin' to ME?
BESS. Well, I—I don't know. If you're Mr. Stiletto, I am.
MICKEY. You are?
BESS. If you're—you're Mr. Stiletto.

(Beat.)

MICKEY. Well, it just so happens I AM Mr. Stiletto.
BESS. Oh. Well, I'm—I'm pleased to—to meet you ...

(SHE offers her hand but of course he can't shake it through the wire. HE stares at her. SHE smiles apologetically.)

MICKEY. Who the fuck are you?

BESS. Ah ... Mr. Rozelli sent me ...

MICKEY. Eddie?

BESS. Yes, he—

MICKEY. You know Eddie?

BESS. Yes, you see, he—

MICKEY. I been standin' here like some dumb SHIT, lookin' for Eddie. So what's the deal? Eddie sent you?

BESS. Yes, he—he did. Won't you sit down?

MICKEY. Oh, yeah. Yeah. *(Sits.)* Had to be sure first. You can't talk to just anybody in this fuckin' place. This is a fuckin' zoo. Y'know? Fuckin' zoo ... So. Eddie sent you. Okay, so what's the juice at Belmont?

BESS. At—at what?

MICKEY. Belmont. What happened last weekend?

(SHE stares at him puzzled.)

MICKEY. Nix it. He prob'ly lost my fuckin' money. So why couldn't Eddie come hisself?

BESS. Well, he—

MICKEY. Cause, you know, Eddie always comes hisself. Two years now, every Tuesday at three o'clock, Eddie comes hisself. Brings me racing tips, cigarettes, gum ... you got any gum?

BESS. No, he—he didn't say anything about any gum; actually, he wanted me to bring you *this.* (*SHE produces a Bible and passes it under the screen to Mickey.*)

MICKEY. What the fuck is this?

BESS. It's—it's a Bible.

MICKEY. What the fuck am I supposed to do with it?

BESS. Well, I think he wanted you to—to—to *read* it.

MICKEY. (*Beat; HE stares at her as if she's from Mars. Then, HE gets it.*) Oh, yeah. Yeah, I get it. Okay. Good. Thanks.

(A BELL rings.)

MICKEY. Oh, hey—I gotta go. Movie in five minutes. Tonight is Marlon Brando in *The Wild One.* (*HE rises.*)

BESS. Oh! Mr. Stiletto—

MICKEY. You tell Eddie I'll see him next Tuesday. Tell him to be on time for once, okay?

BESS. Mr. Stiletto, there's something I have to tell you—! Mr. Stiletto?

(But MICKEY is gone.)

BESS. Oh, dear ...

BLACKOUT

Scene 2

The next Tuesday. BESS is seated as before. MICKEY enters, sees her.

MICKEY. Oh, fuck. Not YOU again! Where the hell is Eddie?

BESS. That's what I tried to tell you last time—

MICKEY. And that fuckin' book you gave me! I ripped the covers off, tore out every single fuckin' page! I couldn't find no money in it nowhere!

BESS. You—ripped the *covers* off?

MICKEY. Yeah.

BESS. You mean, you physically tore it UP?

MICKEY. Yeah.

BESS. A Bible?

MICKEY. Yeah. Wasn't no money hid in it noplace.

BESS. I know I—I could've told you *that*.

MICKEY. Well then what the fuck did you GIVE it to me for if there wasn't no money inside?

BESS. To READ!

(HE looks at her; beat. HE starts to laugh. I mean, really laugh. HE can't stop.)

BESS. I'm sorry you find that so funny, Mr. Stiletto. I mean, I'm really sorry you find that so funny. Maybe if you were on this side of the screen you wouldn't be laughing quite so hard.

MICKEY. (*Stops, ponders the remark.*) Was that a cut?

BESS. The reason I'm here is because ... Mr. Rozelli *hired* me.

MICKEY. Uh-huh ...?

BESS. You see, Mr. Rozelli and I met at the church—

MICKEY. Wait a minute, wait a minute, *wait a minute*. Eddie wasn't inside a no church.

BESS. Yes. He was. I work in the office at St. John's and he came to talk to me about becoming a member—

MICKEY. Hold on a second here; Eddie wanted to join a *church*?

BESS. Yes.

MICKEY. He musta been shittin' you …

BESS. Oh, no. He was very serious. And he told me about you and how you did this big favor for him and ended up here …

MICKEY. Uh-huh …

BESS. He said he felt completely reborn and he wanted you to feel it too. So he hired me to come out here and counsel you.

MICKEY. *Counsel* me?

BESS. Yes.

MICKEY. What is that, like, *teach* me?

BESS. Yes. Exactly.

MICKEY. He hired you to *counsel* me?

BESS. Yes.

(Beat.)

MICKEY. Well then you're fired. Goodbye— *(MICKEY starts to rise.)*

BESS. Mr. Stiletto, wait!

MICKEY. I don't need no counselin'. Now go on back to your church and tell Eddie to get his lousy reborn ass in here before I—

BESS. Eddie Rozelli is dead.

(Beat.)

MICKEY. *What* ...?

BESS. He was stabbed to death in the confessional booth.

MICKEY. Holy fuck ...

BESS. His first confession in twenty-five years.

MICKEY. (*Long pause. MICKEY is stunned.*) So—you're tellin' me ... Eddie ain't comin' up here no more?

(SHE shakes her head "no." Pause.)

MICKEY. I didn't mean what I said. You ain't ... *fired*.

BESS. Thank you, Mr. Stiletto.

MICKEY. Please. Mickey.

BESS. Mickey. (*Takes out another Bible.*) Eddie wanted to give you this. He really did.

(Passes it under the screen. MICKEY takes it.)

BLACKOUT

Scene 3

BESS and MICKEY are seated.. MICKEY beams.

MICKEY. Y'know, that ol' Jesus was a pretty amazin' guy.

BESS. Mmmm ...

MICKEY. Touchin' people and them gettin' healed right off the bat. I mean, shit. The Pope can't even do that!

BESS. So you've been reading the Bible?

MICKEY. Ah ... a little. (*Beat.*) Movie projector's broke down. Prob'ly when it gets fixed, y'know, I won't be readin' so much ...

BESS. I see.

MICKEY. But it fills up my time, y'know, when I ain't down in arts and crafts makin' wallets or some shit. Y'know? I dunno . . . . (*Beat.*) Hey, so what's your story, Bess? You hitched?

BESS. Hitched?

MICKEY. Married. You know.

BESS. Oh, no. No. (*Beat.*) Are you?

MICKEY. Shit no. Not me. Hah. (*Beat.*) Y'know. (*An awkward beat. Then HE reaches into his pocket.*) Hey, listen. For you. (*HE slides something under the screen.*)

BESS. What is it?

MICKEY. Billfold. Made it in arts and crafts.

BESS. (*Reading.*) "E. A." (*Beat.*) These aren't my initials ...

MICKEY. I know, it was gonna be a present for Eddie.

BESS. Oh.

MICKEY. I started it for Eddie. But after you told me he done got stabbed, I *finished* it for you. Was too late to change the initials, y'know, but it's still for you. Here. See them stitches there? I thought a you when I stitched them all in.

BESS. Well ... thank you.

MICKEY. Yeah. Took fuckin' forever.

BESS. Well, thanks.

MICKEY. Ah. What the hell. You know? (*Beat.*) You're welcome.

(*BELL rings.*)

MICKEY. So ... next Tuesday then, huh Bess?
BESS. Yes, Mickey. Next Tuesday.

BLACKOUT

Scene 4

BESS is seated. MICKEY paces, thinking aloud.

MICKEY. Y'know, Bess ... I been thinkin' about Eddie.
BESS. Yes ?
MICKEY. Yeah. And you know how you told me how he done got stabbed in that confession booth?
BESS. Mm-hmm ...
MICKEY. Well, I mean, come on. Who woulda thought a lookin' for *Eddie* in a *church*?
BESS. I don't ... follow you.
MICKEY. I'm sayin'—(*HE looks around.*)—I think it was a inside job. I think somebody on the *inside* did Eddie in.
BESS. The ... inside?
MICKEY. Yeah. You know. One a us.

(Beat.)

BESS. But who would want to kill Eddie? He was such a nice man ...

MICKEY. People got their reasons, Bess. Y'know? Anyway, listen. I want you to do me a favor … I want you to go talk to a fella named Joey Carmello. Here. Here's his business card …

(HE slides it under screen. SHE takes it.)

BESS. It's shaped like a coffin.
MICKEY. He runs a Mortuary out on Grand Avenue. Nice guy. Just tell him what I said. That I think it was a inside job. Tell him I think it was Johnny Perelli.
BESS. Johnny … Perelli?
MICKEY. Yeah. Just tell Joey. He'll know what to do.
BESS. That's all I have to do?
MICKEY. Yeah.
BESS. Go to the mortuary and tell Joey Carmello you think it was Johnny Perelli.
MICKEY. Great.
BESS. Good. *(SHE rises, crosses to door.)*
MICKEY. Hey, Bess?

(SHE stops, turns. Beat. Whatever he was going to say, HE chickens out.)

MICKEY. I'll see you next Tuesday.

BLACKOUT

Scene 5

BESS and MICKEY seated, in the midst of laughter.

MICKEY. I wish they'd lemme have some champagne in here! We'd celebrate!

BESS. So then I helped, huh?

MICKEY. Fuckin'-A Right, you helped! You got Joey to nail old Johnny Perelli. I knew that bastard was up to no good ... Sold real estate for a front. Anybody who sells real estate's got to be up to no good.

BESS. So I'm a hero, huh?

MICKEY. Shit yeah! Johnny Perelli was the one who stabbed Eddie in that confession booth!

BESS. And I helped nab him!

MICKEY. Yeah! You did!

(THEY laugh. After a few moments, it subsides.)

BESS. So what happens now?

MICKEY. What? You mean, to Johnny Perelli?

BESS. Yes. Does he get handed over to the police?

MICKEY. Ah, no. He gets shot fulla holes.

BESS. *(Discouraged.)* Oh ...

MICKEY. Hey, but don't get all sad about it. I mean, shit. This is the MOB.

BESS. I know! You guys keep killing each other; what good does it do?

MICKEY. I dunno.

BESS. What good does it do?

MICKEY. Hey, well don't yell at me, I didn't START it. It started a long time ago.

BESS. I know; I'm sorry. It's just a *disgusting* business. How could anybody choose it for a career?

MICKEY. Ya don't 'xactly choose it. It sorta chooses *you. (Reflective beat.)* Hey. So you can't change the world in a day. It took a week to build Rome, right? What the fuck. You change what you can. You changed Eddie.

BESS. I did?

MICKEY. Yeah. Least you got him to confess 'fore he got killed. He'd a got killed sooner or later. At least this way he ain't burnin' in hell right now.

BESS. Well ...

MICKEY. And look. Me. I only read two books, my whole life, they was both fulla nekkid women. And now—shit! You got me to readin' the fuckin' Bible! *(Beat.)* I shouldn't be sayin' fuck in contest with the Bible, right?

BESS. *(Almost blurted out.)* Mickey, this is my last session.

MICKEY. What?

BESS. Eddie hired me to come out here for twelve sessions.

MICKEY. Yeah?

BESS. This is number twelve.

MICKEY. So?

BESS. I would come out here on my own, but I have to do it as a job through the church so I can come out here during visiting hours and the bus fare all the way out here is more than I can afford and—I'm sorry. If I could I would but I can't so—

MICKEY. So I'll hire you.

BESS. You—what?

MICKEY. I'll hire you. Be my Bible tutor. I'm hirin' you to come out here and counsel me. You tell that church

I'll pay them whatever the fuck they want. (*Looks heavenward.*) Excuse me.

BESS. Are you serious?

MICKEY. 'Course I'm serious. look, you go talk to Joey Carmello. Tell him how much to pay them. He'll take care of it.

BESS. (*Beat. SHE smiles at him.*) Thank you, Mickey.

MICKEY. What, are you shittin' me? Thank YOU.

(BELL rings. SHE rises.)

BESS. So. Next Tuesday then. (*SHE starts to go.*)

MICKEY. Hey Bess—

BESS. (*Almost simultaneous.*) Yes?

MICKEY. I—I read in the Bible you give me, how Jesus went up to them people that was lepers, y'know, and how nobody else'd even touch 'em and he goes up to 'em and heals 'em. (*Beat.*) All my life, anybody halfway decent always done treated me like I was one a those lepers. 'Cept you. That's what made me keep readin'.

BESS. I'm glad you hired me, Mickey.

MICKEY. Me too.

(SHE turns to go.)

MICKEY. Hey, Bess?

BESS. Yes.

MICKEY. I'm gonna get outta here in nine more years, y'know.

BESS. I know. (*Beat. THEY share a warm moment.*) So ... next Tuesday then?

MICKEY. Next Tuesday.

BLACKOUT
End of Play

JOHN'S RING

JOHN'S RING was originally produced in New York by the Dragonfly Theatre Company, Lucas Walker, Artistic Director, at the Sanford Meisner Theatre on October 3, 1985, under the direction of David M. Jaffe. The cast was as follows:

MYRA .... Beth Koules

STELLA ....Navida Stein

AMBER................................. Lori Bashour

The Production Stage Manager was John Mackessy; Lights were designed by Douglas Cox; and Sound was designed by Denise Elkins.

CHARACTERS

MYRA, the oldest. Mid-twenties.

STELLA, the boldest. Mid-twenties.

AMBER, the wealthiest. Early twenties.

SETTING

The action of the play takes place in Myra's Manhattan apartment. 1978.

JOHNS RING

*SCENE: The action takes place in Myra's apartment on the
    Upper West Side of Manhattan.*
One Fall Evening in 1978.

*AT RISE: MYRA is discovered seated on her small sofa,
    watching TV and eating a TV dinner which does not
    look tasty. The DOORBELL rings. SHE goes to the
    door, looks through the peephole, sees who it is, and
    opens the door. Her friends, STELLA and AMBER,
    rush in. BOTH are out of breath, BOTH are
    tremendously excited over something that has just
    happened. THEY pant, out of breath, and vocally
    communicate with either screams or laughter. One
    would swear they were drunk. But they're not.*

MYRA. What? (*STELLA and AMBER gasp.*) What
happened?

(A scream from both girls.)

MYRA. You better hold it down, a buncha old people
live next door.

*(Laughter from BOTH GIRLS. It's clear that they're
    sharing some sort of "inside joke.")*

MYRA. What is it with you two? Have you been to happy hour?

(THEY try to tell her, but start laughing again. THEY are practically shaking with excitement. STELLA points at Amber. THEY both laugh.)

MYRA. What? Did Amber get the job?

(THEY laugh again.)

MYRA. What? Did they hire you, Amber? (*More laughter.*) What is so damn funny? I am beginning to feel left out here.
STELLA. (*To Amber; a gasp.*) Show her!

(AMBER, trembling, reaches into her coat pocket and pulls out a diamond ring. A man's ring. SHE holds it in the air for inspection. STELLA and AMBER scream.)

MYRA. Oh my God! Did Frankie propose? Frankie proposed, didn't he? It's about time—
STELLA. (*To Myra.*) You don't understand, do you?
MYRA. Understand what? Will you tell me what the hell's going on? I can't READ MINDS!
AMBER. (*About the ring, ceremoniously.*) THIS ... is John Lennon's ring.

(Beat. Then AMBER and STELLA scream again.)

MYRA. Will you two quit getting hysterical? That is not John Lennon's ring.

STELLA. How do you know?

MYRA. Well what would you two be doing with John Lennon's ring?

STELLA and AMBER. He gave it to us!!

MYRA. Oh c'mon. Will you TELL me what's going on?

STELLA. (*SHE's coming down by now.*) No, really. This ring belongs—belongED to John Lennon. He gave it to us.

MYRA. When?

AMBER. About an hour ago.

MYRA. How—where? Are you putting me on?

STELLA. Sit down.

(STELLA and AMBER sit MYRA down and proceed to act-out the story.)

STELLA. Okay. Now. Amber and me was walkin' to Rockefeller Center to pick Ma up from work—

AMBER. Yeah.

STELLA. Yeah. And we're walkin' along through the park, 'cause, y'know, it's warm out, an' we're walkin' downtown, an' we get to around Eightieth Street and I say to Amber, "Let's cut over and go by the Dakota."

AMBER. And I say, "Okay." 'Cause you never know, y'know.

STELLA. Yeah, he might be out there.

AMBER. Or even her.

STELLA. Right. So. We cut over to the West Side of the park, and we're walkin' along, and we get to the corner where the Dakota is—

AMBER. —and GUESS WHO IS GETTIN' OUTTA THIS CAB?

MYRA. John Lennon.

STELLA. No. Tommy Wilson.

MYRA. Who?

STELLA. Tommy Wilson. My boyfriend.

MYRA. I thought it was Joey, with the big nose.

STELLA. We broke up. So anyway, I'm talkin' to Tommy, and Amber says to me—

AMBER. "Doesn't that look like—?"

STELLA. —and it was! And we just about shit right there! He was just walkin' along, just like you or me would, all by hisself, and—

AMBER. Lemme tell this part!

STELLA. Okay.

AMBER. Okay. So he's walkin' along, and I say to him, "JOHN! JOHN!"

STELLA. And he stops! And he comes over to us!

AMBER. And I just about wet my pants, I swear! I almost peed! But I held it in!

STELLA. And he says, "How are you girls?"

MYRA. You're kidding!

STELLA. No! And we tell him, y'know, how much we love him and the Beatles—

AMBER. —but we don't talk a lot about the Beatles, 'cause he don't like hearin' all that.

STELLA. So he says somethin' about how great it is to have such devoted fans—do you remember his exact words?

AMBER. No, I was trying not to pee!

MYRA. Where was Tommy all this time?

STELLA. Oh, just standin' there. Tommy lissens to all that weird shit, Sex Pistols and all. I don't think he really knew who John was. Gets me so frustrated, I can't talk Beatles around Tommy. Joey had a big nose, but at least you could talk Beatles to him—

MYRA. So how did he give you the ring?

AMBER. He just did! He said—

STELLA. I remember, I remember, let me tell her!

AMBER. Okay.

STELLA "Well, it's a lovely day to be out and around, darlings. Here."

AMBER. And he handed it to us. And he said—

STELLA. "Something to remember us by." And then he walked off.

MYRA. He said "us?"

STELLA. What?

MYRA. Why did he say "us?"

STELLA. I don't know, it's—what do you call it— when kings and all talk that way, we learned it in school—

AMBER. The Royal "We."

STELLA. That's it. The Royal We. That first person point of view there.

MYRA. That is really incredible. Let me see it.

AMBER. Be careful.

STELLA. Don't scratch it.

MYRA. I won't. (*Examines it.*) Wow. That is really something. John Lennon's ring. (*Beat.*) What did your ma say?

STELLA. Oh no! We forgot about her! Can I use your phone?

MYRA. Sure. If you don't get a dial tone, hit it a coupla times.

STELLA. Okay.

MYRA. How could you forget about your ma?

STELLA. Meeting John would make you forget about anything!

AMBER. We came right over here cause we knew you were the only person that would really just die when we told you.

MYRA. That is really incredible. (*MYRA returns to her TV dinner.*) Yuck. I think these peas are made out of wax.

AMBER. You oughtta go out and eat more.

MYRA. I can't go out and eat.

AMBER. Sure you can.

MYRA. It takes all I make to keep this place. I can't go blowin' money on stuff like food.

AMBER. Oh.

MYRA. And I am not going back home.

AMBER. Oy, I hate home! If I don't get this job, I'll shoot myself. I can't stand this hangin' around the house all the time.

MYRA. You'll get it.

AMBER. I hope so.

MYRA. You'll make a great dental hygienist.

AMBER. It's all I want.

MYRA. You're sharp, Amber. I see you doing great things.

AMBER. You're doin' good.

MYRA. I'm doing okay. Bank Teller's not so great.

AMBER. But you got your own place. That's great.

MYRA. You got the couch whenever you want it. Whenever you get sick of your folks.

AMBER. Thanks.

STELLA. (*Hanging up the phone.*) There's no answer. I hope she gets home okay. I can't believe we just left her there. She's gonna be really pissed!

AMBER. Oy! Last time she got pissed I thought she was gonna throw the TV set out the window!

STELLA. Well you don't hafta keep diggin' that up again and again!

AMBER. I'm not. I'm just sayin' your ma, she's got a temper on her.

STELLA. (*Exploding.*) She works at a newsstand! She gets yelled at all day! She ain't got no husband! What do you expect?

AMBER. Sorry.

(*Beat.*)

STELLA. (*Embarrassed for the outburst.*) Anyway, she'll feel a lot better when I show her the ring.

AMBER. (*An uncomfortable pause. AMBER doesn't quite know how to broach the subject. Then:*) What, are we goin' by your place before I go home?

STELLA. If you want. You can go straight home though. I'll see you tomorrow—

AMBER. But it's my ring.

(*Pause.*)

STELLA. What?
AMBER. It's my ring.
STELLA. How do you figure that?

AMBER. I called him over to start with. He wouldn't have come over if I hadn't taken the initiative. I always take the initiative.

STELLA. But he handed the ring to me.

AMBER. He stuck his hand out. We both grabbed for it.

STELLA. So it's as much mine as it is yours.

AMBER. Where do you come off sayin' it's yours? It's mine.

STELLA. You can't hog it all to yourself. Don't you agree, Myra?

MYRA. (*Her mouth full.*) Hold it. I'm not getting in this thing.

AMBER. You're already in it.

MYRA. How do you figure that?

AMBER. You're the only one who's heard the whole story.

MYRA. I didn't ask to hear it!

STELLA. What do you think? Who should keep the ring?

MYRA. I dunno. I ain't no judge.

STELLA. Tell us, Myra. You always been, like, big sister. What do you think we should do?

MYRA. I dunno. Share it.

AMBER. Share it?

MYRA. Yeah. Take turns.

STELLA. Would you share a husband?

MYRA. What?

STELLA. A husband! Would you share a husband with somebody? It's the same thing!

MYRA. No it's not. It's just a ring.

AMBER. JUST a ring? Did you hear her! It's JOHN'S RING!

MYRA. My Pop would die if he was alive. You know what he'd call you?

STELLA. What?

MYRA. "Starchasers."

AMBER. "Starchasers?"

MYRA. Yeah, that's what you are. You two make this sound like the Second Coming, or something.

AMBER. If it happened to you, you'd see it different.

STELLA. Yeah. Who was the one, waited in line seventeen hours to get seats for Wings Over America at the Garden?

MYRA. That was a long time ago.

AMBER. A year and a half ago.

STELLA. Yeah.

MYRA. So?

STELLA. You used to worship them, just like us! Beatles Forever, remember?

AMBER. We sat together at Shea Stadium!

STELLA. You screamed louder than botha us put together!

MYRA. I was only twelve then!

AMBER. So?

STELLA. What I'M sayin' is, if this happened to you, you'd act the same way. So put yourself in our place and be the judge.

MYRA. I don't wanna be the judge.

AMBER. Who else are we gonna ask?

STELLA. Yeah. Ma's gonna say we're bein' silly.

AMBER. Yeah. You help us decide.

MYRA. Okay, okay. If I decide for you, will you let me eat in peace?

STELLA. Okay.

AMBER. Okay.

(Pause. MYRA tries to figure out how to go about this thing. The others wait. Long silence.)

AMBER. So? Who gets the ring?

MYRA. Will you wait a second? I'm trying to think of something.

AMBER. Well think faster.

MYRA. Okay, okay. Here. Give me the ring.

AMBER. Here.

MYRA. Okay. We're gonna have an auction.

STELLA. An auction?

MYRA. Yeah. And you'll both bid for it.

AMBER. Okay!

STELLA. That is no fair! You know I'm broke She's got money comin' out her ass—!

AMBER. Watch your language!

STELLA. Well it's not fair! We don't even have a car, they just got three! They're rolling in money! I lose that one before we even start!

MYRA. Well then we won't use money.

AMBER. What?

MYRA. We'll have an auction, but we won't use money.

AMBER. What'll we use, then?

MYRA. Your purses. Empty them out.

STELLA. Myra!

MYRA. Go ahead, dump them out!

AMBER. Why?
MYRA. Just do it!

(THEY do so.)

MYRA. Now. You'll bid for the ring using the stuff in your purses. No money.
AMBER. That's stupid.
MYRA. I think it's a great idea.
AMBER. Well I think it's ridiculous.
MYRA. Do you want the fucking ring?
AMBER. Yes!
MYRA. Then bid, dammit! The bidding is open!

(The auction begins. There is lots of concentration here. Each GIRL carefully studies her opponent's move and thoughtfully counters. The whole thing takes on the weight and feel of a championship chess game with high stakes.)

STELLA. I bid one melted Reese cup.
MYRA. See now? That's a good start. Amber?
AMBER. Oh, I can beat that. Here. A package of Juicy Fruit.
STELLA. Binaca Breath Spray.
AMBER. I raise you a spray can of Mace.
STELLA. A pencil.
AMBER. A pen. Gold. My dad's.
STELLA. A pamphlet.
AMBER. A book.
STELLA. Paper clips.
AMBER. A stapler!

STELLA. (*Gasping at straws now.*) YWCA Card!

AMBER. (*Triumphant.*) Master Card!

STELLA. That is no fair!

AMBER. Yes it is!

STELLA. Miss Nouveau Riche, always flaunting her wealth!

AMBER. So?

STELLA. Everybody knows your folks just came into that! They laugh at you! You're like a buncha parasites!

AMBER. Don't call us parasites! At least I got a father!

MYRA. Guys!

STELLA and AMBER. What?

MYRA. Cool it!

AMBER. Well it was your idea to start with Myra!

STELLA. Yeah.

AMBER. So who gets the ring?

MYRA. What?

STELLA. Who gets the ring?

MYRA. I don't know ...

AMBER. Of course you don't know. You got a tabletop full of crap, how can that tell you anything?

STELLA. Yeah, you're treating us like children.

MYRA. Well you're acting like children. I don't see what the big deal is. Share the damn ring.

STELLA. You would NOT say that if YOU had been there today. YOU would be one of us, fighting for this ring!

MYRA. I would not. In the end, what difference does it make WHO keeps the ring?

STELLA. It is a SPIRITUAL difference! It matters down inside!

MYRA. You're just downright selfish.

STELLA. I am not! Look, you can pretend lt doesn't matter, but I know it does. It matters to you! It's just an act, the way you pretend you're so superior.

MYRA. I do NOT pretend I'm superior.

AMBER. Yes you do. Ever since you moved here. She's right, you know. It's all affected. Bein' surrounded by all these luxuries, you THINK you've changed, but you're still just like you were, inside.

MYRA. LUXURIES? You call this a LUXURY? I got no hot water. I'm eating a 79-cent TV dinner that tastes like ear wax. This is not luxuries, kids.

STELLA. "KIDS!" Did you hear that? She's lookin' down on us!

MYRA. I am not!

AMBER. I don't wanna talk about it! I'm goin' home!

STELLA. Wait a minute! Gimme the ring first.

AMBER. I am NOT giving you this ring. This is my ring!

STELLA. No, it's MY ring!

AMBER. I am keeping this ring!

STELLA. No, I am keeping this ring!

AMBER. Give it here!

STELLA. No!

AMBER. If you don't give it here, I'll tell Tommy how much you REALLY weigh.

STELLA. If you do, I'll tell Frank where you were last weekend!

AMBER. Give me the ring!

STELLA. No!

MYRA. (*Jumping up and grabbing it.*) SHUT UP and give me the damn ring!

AMBER. What are you—?

STELLA. —where are you goin' with that?

(MYRA runs into the bathroom and slams the door shut behind her, locking it.)

STELLA. What are you doing?

MYRA. *(From within.)* If you two don't stop fighting and agree to share the ring, I'm gonna flush it down the toilet!

STELLA. NO! NO! Don't do that!

AMBER. PLEASE! DON'T! PLEASE!

MYRA. I will. Now promise you'll share the ring and I'll bring it out. *(Pause.)* Promise.

STELLA. Okay, we promise ...

AMBER. We promise.

MYRA. I don't believe you. Say it in unison. Say it. Pledge it. Say, "We promise ..."

STELLA and AMBER. "We promise ..."

MYRA. "... we will share the ring."

STELLA and AMBER. "... we will share the ring."

(Pause.)

STELLA. You comin' out?

MYRA. No. I still don't believe you.

(Pause.)

AMBER. I have twenty dollars If I slide it under the door, will you give me the ring?

STELLA. Hey, that's not fair! I don't have any money!

AMBER. And I'll slide my dad's credit card under the door.

(Pause.)

MYRA. Which store?

AMBER. Bloomie's.

STELLA. THAT IS NOT FAIR!!

AMBER. Is it a deal? I'll throw in Macy's too! (*No answer.*) Myra? Is it a deal?

(The TOILET flushes. STELLA and AMBER freeze. MYRA emerges. SHE does not have the ring.)

MYRA. (*After a long, tense pause.*) One day you'll thank me. If I gave it to either of you, you'd never forgive me.

STELLA. Thanks a lot.

AMBER. That really sucks.

STELLA. I hate you!

AMBER. I will never speak to you again!

MYRA. Yes you will. When you cool off.

AMBER. I will never cool off! John Lennon does not give rings away every day!

STELLA. Yeah!

MYRA. I really think it's best that neither of you kept that ring.

AMBER. Well good for you. Let's go Stella.

STELLA. I'm with you.

AMBER. I think we should go get drunk and listen to *Abbey Road* and cry.

STELLA. Yeah.

AMBER. (*At the door now.*) I do hope you will be able to live with yourself now, Myra. John will never forgive you.

STELLA. Yeah. I hope you choke on that TV dinner.

(*And THEY are gone. MYRA paces about the room for a few moments in silence. Then, SHE reaches into her pocket and pulls it out. The ring. SHE gazes at it a moment, then bursts into a victorious scream.*)

BLACKOUT

NIGHTS IN HOHOKUS

Nights in Hohokus was originally produced in New York by the Dragonfly Theatre Company, Lucas Walker, Artistic Director, at the Riverwest Theatre on June 17, 1987 under the direction of Angelo Tiffe. The cast was as follows:

LENNY .... Kevin Cristaldi

MANNY .... David M. Jaffe

The Production Stage Manager was Leah Schneider; Lights were designed by Karl E. Haas; Set Design was by Lucas Walker; and Sound was designed by Brenton P. Evans.

CHARACTERS

LENNY—Late 20s. Restless, anxious to go somewhere in life, but the safety of the past pulls on him.

MANNY—Late 20s. A few years ago, he was probably the life of the party. Now he's a chronic complainer. If he could sit in this bar twenty-four hours a day, he would. He has a sliver of metal in his right hand. It's 1/16" long, by the way.

SETTING

Late Summer, the present. A bar in New Jersey.

NIGHTS IN HOHOKUS

Scene 1

SCENE: The suggestion of a bar in New Jersey: a table center stage with a pitcher of beer and two mugs, maybe a bowl of pretzels. Perhaps a jukebox, pinball machine or a Neon Bud sign in the background. A haze permeates the whole bar.

A period of several days exists in between each scene; each blackout should be very staccatto and each time the lights come up, LENNY and MANNY should be in different positions from the previous scene and, if possible, in a slight change of clothing.

LENNY. Manny ...
MANNY. Lenny ...
LENNY. So tell me what's shakin'.
MANNY. Same old shit ...
LENNY. Yeah, I hear ya.
MANNY. Just kickin' around, you know.
LENNY. I hear ya.
MANNY. Drawin' my check.
LENNY. I hear ya. (*Pause; THEY eat some pretzels.*)
You see the Mets last night?
MANNY. Mets?
LENNY. Yeah. On TV.
MANNY. Last night?
LENNY. Yeah.

MANNY. Mets play last night?
LENNY. Yeah.
MANNY. Oh.
LENNY. Yeah.

(Beat.)

MANNY. Naw, I didn't see 'em. *(Pause.)* Shit!
LENNY. What?
MANNY. What's today?
LENNY. Sunday.
MANNY. Shit!
LENNY. What?
MANNY. You know what *tomorrow* is!

(Beat.)

LENNY. Monday …?
MANNY. Shit!
LENNY. What?
MANNY. That pisses me off.
LENNY. What does?
MANNY. Standin' in that *line* every other fuckin' Monday!
LENNY. Line?
MANNY. Yeah.
LENNY. What line?
MANNY. To draw my check.
LENNY. Oh.
MANNY. Yeah. All them deadbeats. Low-lifes.
LENNY I know.
MANNY. They don't *deserve* that money.

LENNY. I hear ya.

MANNY. What the fuck, I mean, guys like you an' me, we've *worked*, y'know? They owe us.

LENNY. I hear ya.

MANNY. But *some* a those people ...

LENNY. I know.

MANNY. You know?

LENNY. I hear ya.

MANNY. I know. (*Beat.*) So who won?

LENNY. Won?

MANNY. Mets game. Who were they playin'?

LENNY. Dodgers, I think it was.

MANNY. So who won?

LENNY. I dunno. I fell asleep before it was over. Extra innings.

MANNY. Oh.

LENNY. Yeah.

(*Beat.*)

MANNY. How 'bout before you fell asleep?

LENNY. Huh?

MANNY. Before you fell asleep. You remember who was winnin' then?

LENNY. Mets, I think. Mets had the lead.

MANNY. Good.

LENNY. Yeah.

(*Beat.*)

MANNY. Hey Lenny.

LENNY. Yeah?

MANNY. Can you give me a ride home?
LENNY. A ride?
MANNY. Yeah. When you leave here tonight.

(Beat.)

LENNY. A ride *home*?
MANNY. Yeah. *(Beat.)* I can't drive.
LENNY Can't drive?
MANNY. Naw.
LENNY. Why? Did they take away your license again?
MANNY. Naw, man. I haven't been able to drive since—*(HE holds up his right hand.)*—you know.
LENNY. Oh.
MANNY. Yeah. *(Beat.)* So ... ?
LENNY. So?
MANNY. Can I have a ride home?

(Long, long *pause.)*

LENNY. Yeah, Manny. You can have a ride.

BLACKOUT

Scene 2

MANNY. So I go home with this girl, see? And we're talkin, y'know, she's givin me a hand job and I tell this girl, see, she says so where are you from and I tell her, I say I'm from Hohokus.

LENNY. Yeah?

MANNY. And she starts *laughin'*!

LENNY. Yeah?

MANNY. Yeah! Right inna middle of a hand job, she laughs!

LENNY. Really?

MANNY. Yeah! I hate it when people laugh! I mean, what the fuck is so funny about Hohokus, right?

LENNY. I know.

MANNY. You know?

LENNY. Yeah.

MANNY. She thinks she's so hot, she got her this little Mexican dog—whattya call those?

LENNY. Chihuahuas.

MANNY. Yeah. Them little things that look like rats.

LENNY. Yeah.

MANNY. Yeah. And she's got this dog and she's named it "Morton." I mean, come *on*. And she's actin' like she's so goddamn uppity. But I showed her.

LENNY. You did?

MANNY. Yeah.

LENNY. So what'd you do?

MANNY. To the girl?

LENNY. Yeah.

MANNY. I threw that fuckin' dog out the window!

LENNY. No!

MANNY. Yeah!

LENNY. Yeah?

MANNY. Damn right I did!   Anybody laughs at Hohokus, what the fuck do they expect!

LENNY. I guess so.

MANNY. I mean, you know?

LENNY. Sure I know.
MANNY. I know.

(Beat. THEY drink.)

MANNY. So what's, like, *new* in your life?
LENNY. Not much.
MANNY. Me neither.
LENNY. I think … well, I think I may a found a job.
MANNY. A job?
LENNY. Yeah. Finally.
MANNY. You found a job?
LENNY. Well, *maybe*, yeah …
MANNY. Maybe?
LENNY. Yeah. *(Beat.)* But I'm not *sure* yet.

(Beat .)

MANNY. What kinda job?
LENNY. Maintenance.
MANNY. Maintenance?
LENNY. Yeah. You know.
MANNY. What sorta maintenance?
LENNY. At the Meadowlands.
MANNY. Meadowlands?
LENNY. Yeah. You know. Giants Stadium—
MANNY. I *know* Giants Stadium, dipshit!
LENNY. Okay!
MANNY. I mean, we *both* know Giants Stadium!
LENNY. Okay!

(Pause.)

MANNY. 'At's a good job.

LENNY. Yeah?

MANNY. Yeah. It's a union job, right?

LENNY. I dunno.

MANNY. Well if it's it a *stadium*, for chrissakes—

LENNY. I dunno, okay?

MANNY. What, they're givin' you a job and you don't even know if it's union job?

LENNY. I didn't say they was givin' it to me; I said I think they *may* be gonna give it to me! I won't know for a coupla *weeks*—

MANNY. Well what kinda job is it?

(Beat.)

LENNY. Never mind.

MANNY. What *kind*?

LENNY. Don't matter—

MANNY. Tell me.

LENNY. It don't make no difference—

MANNY. What the fuck is wrong with you?

LENNY. I haven't even got it yet!

MANNY. I mean, what the *fuck*?

LENNY. Shuttup, everybody's lookin' *over* here, man—

MANNY. Will you just fuckin tell me and quit worryin' about everybody *else*—?

LENNY. *Groomin' the astroturf!*

(Dead silence.)

MANNY. Astroturf?

LENNY. Yes.

MANNY. (*Chuckling and savoring the phrase.*) The Astroturf Groomer!

LENNY. Shuttup!

MANNY. (*To the bar.*) Ladies and Gentlemen, Lenny Morales, The Astroturf Groomer!

LENNY. (*Sinking into the chair.*) Jesus!

MANNY. (*To Lenny.*) What a motherfuckin' pansy-ass job.

LENNY. Well at least it's a *job*!

(*Pause.*)

MANNY. Well ... I can't do just *any* job.

(*MANNY holds his hand up. LENNY looks at it.*)

MANNY. You know?

LENNY. (*Under his breath.*) I know ...

MANNY. You *know*?

LENNY. (*Losing patience.*) I *know*!

BLACKOUT

Scene 3

Silence. Both LENNY and MANNY sit still. MANNY begins to laugh at some thought or other. LENNY

looks at him. MANNY stops. LENNY looks away.
MANNY starts laughing again.

LENNY. What is so goddamn funny all of a sudden?

MANNY. I was just thinkin ...

LENNY. That's not funny, that's fuckin *tragic*.

MANNY. No, I was just wonderin' like, what does an Astroturf Groomer *do*?

LENNY. Jesus H. Christ.

MANNY. No, I wanna know.

LENNY. I never shoulda told you.

MANNY. Why not?

LENNY. 'Cause. It's probably gonna jinx it for me.

MANNY. Jinx it?

LENNY. Yeah.

MANNY. Tellin' *me* is gonna *jinx* it?

LENNY. Maybe.

MANNY. You're fuckin crazy.

LENNY. No, it might.

MANNY. Fuckin' crazy!

LENNY. Lotta times, I tell people things that I hope will happen before they happen, and—phht!—they get screwed all up. Y'know. Jinxed.

MANNY. Not with me.

LENNY. Maybe ...

MANNY. Not me. I'm not a fuckin' jinxer.

LENNY. Yeah you are.

MANNY. I am not!

LENNY. Just let's forget it, okay—?

MANNY. What have I jinxed?

LENNY. Manny—

MANNY. No, tell me one thing that you done told me before that I jinxed up for you.

LENNY. Shirley Pirelli.

(Beat.)

MANNY. What?

LENNY. You 'member that night I was plannin' to poke Shirley Pirelli?

MANNY. Yeah ...

LENNY. An' I *told* you before I went over there that I was plannin' to poke her ...?

MANNY. Yeah?

LENNY. So then, there it was.

(Beat.)

MANNY. There *what* was?

LENNY. I get over there, and Shirley Pirelli is on the rag.

(Beat.)

MANNY. Wait a minute, you're tryin' to tell me that by you tellin' me that you was gonna do Shirley Pirelli, that was the reason she was on the *rag*?

LENNY. Yeah.

MANNY. You're sayin' it was *my fault* she was on the rag?

LENNY. If it wasn't yours, then whose was it?

MANNY. Christ, I dunno Lenny. It wasn't my fault. If it was anybody's fault, it was *God*'s fault—

LENNY. Hey! Don't start talkin' about God, Manny. Sister Katherine warned you about talkin' about God.

MANNY. Yeah ... well, I *poked* Sister Katherine.

(Pause.)

LENNY. You ... *what*?

MANNY. Yeah.

LENNY. You?

MANNY. Yeah.

LENNY. Poked a *nun*?

MANNY. Yeah.

LENNY. Oh my God, Manny. When?

MANNY. Well let's not make a whole big fuckin' *deal* out of it—

LENNY. Manny, it already is a big fuckin' deal, don't you know you're probably gonna burn in *hell* for that?

MANNY. Naw. She was a *nun*! *(Beat.) Think* about it!

(Beat.)

LENNY. Manny, what is a nun like—?

MANNY. Hey, what the fuck, I don't give out the intimate details of my private sexual life—

LENNY. Since when?

MANNY. Since—what do you mean, since when? I don't go around, tellin' everybody about the women I ball!

LENNY. Yeah you do!

MANNY. I do not! *(Beat.)* Maybe once or twice, I did. *(Beat.)* Not often.

LENNY. Manny, you used to sell Polaroid pictures of the girls you poked.

MANNY. That was a long time ago. In my *youth*. (*Beat*.) I can't do stuff like that no more. I can't do ... a lotta stuff no more on account a I got—

LENNY.—you got a sliver in your hand, yeah, yeah, I *know* already! Fuckin' sliver in your hand keeps you from doin' *everything*!

MANNY. Well, that's an asshole thing to say. (*Pause*.) Asshole!

BLACKOUT

Scene 4

MANNY. *You* try goin' through life with a metal sliver in your hand two inches long.

LENNY. Two inches?

MANNY. Yeah.

LENNY. They said it was an eighth of an inch.

MANNY. It *grows*, Lenny.

LENNY. Jesus.

MANNY. It does. Every day, I can feel it, you know, like, *expandin'*. I can hardly make a fist anymore. Look: see? Can't go bowlin' no more ... can't pick up the goddamn ball.

LENNY. You never could bowl worth a shit anyway.

MANNY. Says *you*. (*Belch*.) Fuckin' Astroturf.

LENNY. Shuttup about the astroturf, okay? I still haven't even heard if I *got* it—

MANNY. Ooh, then I better shuttup, before I *jinx* it for you. (*Beat*.) I'm gonna come out there when you start workin'. And I'm gonna sit in section EE, just like we used to with Panko, and yell at you while you're paintin' stripes on the fake fuckin' grass!

LENNY. I wish Panko was around to hear this shit you're givin' me.

MANNY. Well he ain't.

LENNY. He'd kick your ass.

MANNY. Well he ain't *here*.

BLACKOUT

Scene 5

MANNY. Y'know ... we oughtta go up and see Panko one a these days.

LENNY. I ain't goin' up there.

MANNY. C'mon ...

LENNY. I'm not.

MANNY. It's *Panko* for chrissakes!

LENNY. I don't care if it's the fuckin' Pope. I ain't goin' up there no more. I *hate* goin' up there ...

MANNY. Why? We'll get us some beer—

LENNY. I hate drivin' all the way out there and I hate sittin on the hood of my car and I hate watchin Panko work on the highway layin' asphalt with the *rest* a those fuckin' jailbirds!

(Pause.)

MANNY. Some friend you are.

LENNY. I hate it.

MANNY. His wife would like us to go.

LENNY. Tell her to go herself.

MANNY She's gonna have a kid, Lenny.

LENNY. It ain't Panko's.

MANNY. How do you know?

LENNY. Panko's been in the slammer for two years, how the hell could it be his?

MANNY. We should respect her wishes, y'know.

LENNY. She's a hose, Manny!

MANNY. C'mon! You gotta go! You gotta drive! (*Holds up his hand.*)

LENNY. What, that's still keepin' you from *drivin'*?

MANNY. Yeah!

LENNY. Jesus!

MANNY. It *does*! I'll be drivin' along and I can feel it start ... *expandin'*—you know, growing. And it makes my hand go into all kindsa convulsions ... Like this: (*HE demonstrates.*)

LENNY. Shuttup.

MANNY. You don't believe me?

LENNY. I believe you.

MANNY. You don't believe me.

LENNY. I believe you, okay? I fuckin' *believe* you.

BLACKOUT

Scene 6

MANNY. I shoulda won that case.

LENNY. Well ...

MANNY. Got me a good lawyer off that TV commercial. Shit, it was an open-and-shut case! Fuckin' Japanese company puts a metal sliver in my hand, they oughta own up to it!

LENNY. It wasn't their fault.

MANNY. The fuck it wasn't their fault! It was their toaster oven!

LENNY. But you didn't buy it, Manny!

MANNY. I had *business* with it.

LENNY. You was usin' it to beat up on Tommy Scarzelli.

MANNY. I was usin' it to pound some sense into him. He owed me money. (*Beat.*) Anybody in their right mind woulda done the same thing. (*Beat.*) Fuckin' Japanese machines. How did I know it'd break into a million pieces.

LENNY. Well you're lucky Tommy Scarzelli didn't fuckin' die!

MANNY Are you kiddin' me? *He's* lucky he didn't fuckin' die! I shoulda punched his lights out for good, just like Panko did that guy from Philadelphia!

LENNY. He owed you two hundred bucks. It ain't worth killin' somebody over two hundred bucks!

MANNY. I *needed* the money!

LENNY. Manny, if you could look at it, you'd see what you done wasn't right!

MANNY. Oh, we're into *morals* now! (*To the bar.*) Astroturf Groomers got all *kindsa* fuckin' morals!

LENNY. It *wasn't* right! You walked into Crazy Eddie's appliance department where he worked, picked up a toaster oven from offa the display, and beat the shit outta him with it!

MANNY. I beat the shit outta him with my hand, big shot! My *hand*! Fuckin' Japanese toaster oven fell all to pieces when I hit him with it!

LENNY. What the fuck, who cares?

MANNY. I care, Lenny! I got a stainless steel sliver in my hand from that goddamn Japanese toaster oven—it's fucked up my whole life! I can't make no fist!

LENNY. Well, you can make fuckin' *excuses*!

MANNY. What the fuck is *that* supposed ta mean?

LENNY. It means you got a sliver all right! In your fuckin' *brain*!

(Silence. THEY sit still. MANNY grimaces in pain.)

MANNY. Jesus Christ, where are my fuckin' Rolaids?

LENNY. How the hell should I know?

MANNY. Shuttup.

LENNY. Check your pocket.

MANNY. Fuck my pocket!

LENNY. Fuck you!

MANNY. Christ, I'm outta Rolaids.

LENNY. So?

MANNY. I got fuckin' heartburn that'd kill a goddamn *elephant*! *(Beat.)* Shit. You got any Rolaids?

LENNY. No.

MANNY. Bullshit! You *always* got Rolaids!

LENNY. Not anymore.

MANNY. What, you don't carry Rolaids no more?

LENNY. No.

MANNY. What, you don't get fuckin' heartburn no more?

LENNY. No.

MANNY. You used to. Alla time!

LENNY. Well I don't got it no more, okay?

MANNY. Oh, then I guess I'll hafta become a fuckin' Astroturf Groomer! Cure my heartburn! *(To the bar.)* Didja hear that, everybody? Groomin' Astroturf is a cure for *heartburn!*

LENNY. Will you sit down and shuttup? I ain't got no Rolaids and I ain't got no heartburn.

MANNY. That's cause you don't have a sliver in your hand—

LENNY. *(In one breath.)* WILL YOU SHUT THE FUCK UP ABOUT THE GODDAMN SLIVER ALREADY? I *KNOW* YOU GOT THE SLIVER! YOU DONE TOLD ME SIXTEEN TIMES A DAY FOR THE LAST YEAR AND A HALF THAT YOU GOT THE GODDAMN SLIVER! I KNOW BY NOW THAT YOU GOT A FUCKIN' SLIVER IN YOUR GODDAMN FUCKIN' HAND, *OKAY?*

(Pause.)

MANNY. But you don't got no Rolaids?

(Pause.)

LENNY. No.

BLACKOUT

Scene 7

MANNY. So, we goin' Monday?
LENNY. Monday?
MANNY. Yeah.
LENNY. What's Monday?
MANNY. It's when we're goin'.
LENNY. Goin' where?
MANNY. Ta see Panko.
LENNY. Oh.

(Beat.)

MANNY. I called the jail, told 'im we was comin'.
LENNY. You *called* 'im?
MANNY. Yeah. (*Chuckles.*) Fuckin' asshole wants us ta bring him a carton a cigarettes. He says ta me, he says, *"anything* without a filter." On account a they give 'em cigarettes in there that's all filtered-up. I dunno *why*. Panko didn't know why neither, but he wanted some filter-less cigarettes. I told him—
LENNY. I got that job, Manny.
MANNY. Job?
LENNY. Yeah.
MANNY. What job?
LENNY. Ah … at Giants Stadium.
MANNY. Oh! Mr. *Astroturf!*
LENNY. Shut up.
MANNY. Mr. *Groomer!*
LENNY. I never shoulda told you.

MANNY. What a dipshit word: groomer. Who the fuck thought of that word? Who the fuck thinks of words anyway, you ever think a that—?

LENNY.—I start on Monday.

(Pause.)

MANNY. You can't start on Monday.

LENNY. Why not?

MANNY. We're goin' ta see Panko Monday. *(Pause.)* Ain't we goin'? We're goin' ta see Panko, aren't we? Ain't that what you said?

LENNY. I never said *I* was goin'!

MANNY. Some friend *you* are!

(Beat.)

MANNY. Some fuckin' friend!

LENNY. So what the fuck do you consider bein a friend? Huh? Wastin' away the rest a my life sittin' in this fuckin' bar, hearin' about your goddamn *sliver*—?

MANNY. I don't talk about my sliver all that much! *(Beat.)* I don't!

LENNY. That ain't the point, Manny—

MANNY. So you're afraid you gonna be stuck with me? You're lucky you got me, I'm the only friend you got!

LENNY. And that's what's depressin' me!

MANNY. Well don't worry about it. Panko'll be out soon and it'll be the three of us, like it used to!

LENNY. Manny, Panko ain't comin' back—

MANNY. The fuck you say!

LENNY. He ain't!

MANNY. Fuck you!
LENNY. Manny—
MANNY. Panko is comin back!
LENNY. He got *life,* Manny.

(Pause.)

MANNY. No, see—he's gonna get out for good behavior.

(Pause.)

LENNY. Panko? Panko ain't got a ounce a good behavior in his whole fuckin' *body*!
MANNY. He's changed!
LENNY. No.
MANNY. He has! He told me!
LENNY. Manny, just last month he bit a guard.
MANNY. That was a relapse.
LENNY. He ain't gettin' out, Manny—
MANNY. Lenny—
LENNY. He *killed* a guy, Manny. (*Beat.*) He killed a guy. He done it and that's it. We gotta let go a him, he ain't comin' back.
MANNY. You just wait and see. Panko and me'll get things goin' again and it'll be just like it used to be. Better! And you'll be cryin' in your beer cause you shunned me! Shunned a guy with A SLIVER IN HIS HAND! (*Pause.*) See? I don't talk about it all that much. I just mentioned it once all day today. (*Long pause.*) Okay, twice.

BLACKOUT

Scene 8

A good bit of time has passed; LENNY now wears a Giants shirt or jacket—something with a logo on it.

LENNY. So. How you been?
MANNY. Okay.
LENNY. Yeah?
MANNY. Yeah ...

(Pause.)

LENNY. You go see Panko?
MANNY. Panko?
LENNY. Yeah.
MANNY. Nah ... I didn't go.
LENNY. No?
MANNY. How'm I supposed ta get there? Y'know ...
(Holds up his hand.)
LENNY. Oh. Yeah.

(Pause.)

MANNY. So .... how's the astroturf look?
LENNY. Good. Real good. Gonna be a good season.
MANNY. Yeah?
LENNY. Yeah.

(Pause.)

MANNY. 'Member when you and me and Panko used to go out there?
LENNY. Yeah.

(Beat.)

MANNY. Sittin' out in section EE.
LENNY. Yeah ...
MANNY. Lookin' at the girls .
LENNY. Yeah ...
MANNY. Trippin' the hot dog vendors.

(No answer from LENNY. Pause.)

MANNY. Maybe I'll come out there one a these days.
LENNY. I bet I can getcha in free.
MANNY. Yeah?
LENNY. Probably.

(Beat.)

MANNY. I can't go out there.
LENNY. Why not?
MANNY. Can't drive.
LENNY. So. Take a bus.
MANNY. A bus?
LENNY. Yeah.
MANNY. I ain't ridin' on no bus! Fuckin' faggots ride on busses!
LENNY. So then sit at home, I don't care!

(Pause.)

MANNY. *(Cautiously.)* They got a bus that goes all the way out there?
LENNY. Yeah.
MANNY. All the way to the door?
LENNY. I guess so, yeah.
MANNY. Imagine that.
LENNY. Yeah.
MANNY. Fuckin' bus …
LENNY. Uh-huh …

(Beat.)

MANNY. I might do that then, sometime. *(Long pause.)* Y'know somethin', Lenny?
LENNY. Hmm?
MANNY. I miss the old days.
LENNY. I know, Manny. So do I.

(Pause.)

MANNY. Did I tell ya? I hit some guy the other day.
LENNY. Yeah?
MANNY. Yeah. Guy over at McSorley's?
LENNY. What for?
MANNY. He laughed when I said where I was from.
LENNY. Hohokus.
MANNY. Yeah. I said Hohokus and he starts laughin' so I busted his nose for him. Stupid shit.

(Pause.)

MANNY. You make sure that astroturf's all green when I come out there, Lenny.

LENNY. I'll make sure of it, Manny.

MANNY. (*Pause. MANNY looks around the bar, takes it all in.*) Y'know ... Hohokus ain't a bad place, Lenny.

LENNY. No it's not, Manny. (*Beat.*) Hohokus ain't a bad place at all.

BLACKOUT

End of Play

SUGGESTED BREAKDOWN FOR
PERFORMING ALL FIVE PLAYS

ACTOR 1   Jim, *Shoes*
                       Joey, *Best Warm Beer*
                       Mickey, *Next Tuesday*

ACTOR 2   Tony, *Shoes*
                       Eddie, *Best Warm Beer*

ACTOR 3   Manny, *Nights in Hohokus*
                       Tex, *Best Warm Beer*

ACTOR 4   Foreigner, *Shoes*
                       Lenny, *Nights in Hohokus*

ACTRESS 1   Bess, *Next Tuesday*
                       Amber, *John's Ring*

ACTRESS 2   Myra, *John's Ring*

ACTRESS 3   Stella, *John's Ring*

AUTHOR'S NOTES

Just a brief word about *Nights in Hohokus* and *Next Tuesday*.

First of all, and I suppose this may be obvious, the most important thing to address, I think, in doing these two pieces, is to "flavor" each scene as distinctly as possible—to make sure there is a completely different mood in each successive scene from the one before. Each scene takes place on a different day and time and that must be communicated to the audience. *Be specific*. What day is it, what time, etc. This helps reinforce to the audience that time is passing without undergoing numerous costume changes. When *Nights in Hohokus* was first produced, however, we found it a good idea to have Lenny quickly change shirts during *some* of the blackouts to reinforce the passage of time; as the play progressed, he began to look a little nicer. Manny, of course, stayed the same. Don't get too fancy, though. The important thing is not to make Lenny look different, but to make the blackouts as fast as possible and get on with the story. Another nice stunt in Hohokus: our director Angelo Tiffe came up with what I thought was a neat device: a fake tabletop which was absolutely covered with turned-over empty bottles, filled ashtrays, etc. During one of the blackouts, this fake tabletop was plopped down on Lenny and Manny's table and when the lights came up they played the scene as if it were three in the morning and they were drunk as hell. Then, next scene, the tabletop was clear again, it was four o'clock one afternoon, and they were sober.

In presenting *Next Tuesday*, we elected to keep each character in his or her original costume for the duration of the play, focusing even more intensely on the specific mood and circumstances of each scene to reveal the passage of time. This is a bit easier in *Next Tuesday* as a blossoming romance implies a progression in time.

One last note, about *all* the plays. Some of these characters may not have all the "smarts" in the world, they may not be brain surgeons. But don't play them as caricatures. They're sincere in their wishes, dreams, and desires, no matter how weird these may at times seem.

COSTUME PLOT

Shoes

JIM
White shirt
Black work pants
Apron
Black work shoes

TONY
Cheap suit
Tie
Dress shirt
Dress shoes

FOREIGNER
Worn, ragged suit
Soiled dress shirt

The Best Warm Beer in Brooklyn

JOEY
White shirt
Black work pants
Black cop shoes
White bartender's apron

EDDIE
Wrinkled, worn suit
Soiled shirt
Frayed tie

Scuffed dress shoes
White socks

Next Tuesday

MICKEY
Prison shirt with number stenciled on
Prison pants
Boots
White t-shirt

BESS
Simple cotton dress
Dress shoes

John's Ring

MYRA
Oversized sweatshirt
Jeans
Socks

STELLA
Inexpensive cotton print dress
Clogs

AMBER
Nice sweater
Slacks
Sneakers
Jewelry

Nights in Hohokus

MANNY
Worn khaki work pants
Work boots
Old white v-neck t-shirt

LENNY
Jeans
Work boots
Beer logo t-shirt
Giants shirt (Scene 8)

PROPERTY LIST

Shoes

Lunch counter
Stools
Tables and chairs
Silverware
Glasses
Coffee cups & saucers
Coffee pot
Cash register
Chalkboard with "Today's Specials"
Assorted diner counter dressing (optional):
    Bowl of mints
    Gum or candy display
    Menu rack
    Plastic plants
Assorted dressing for tables:
    Napkin dispensers
    Salt & pepper shakers
    Sugar packets & containers
    Cream containers
    Ketchup bottles
    Ashtrays
Broom
Dustpan
Newspaper (Tony)
Paper with English expressions (Foreigner)
Bus ticket (Foreigner)
Letter in envelope (Jim)

The Best Warm Beer in Brooklyn

Bar
Barstools
Tables and chairs
Jukebox (optional)
Standing floor fan
Extension cord
Silverware
Assorted beer mugs & glasses
Bar towels & cleaning rags
Bottled beer (Budweiser)
Beer nuts
Wallet (Joey)
Photo of Rosa (in Joey's wallet)
Publisher's letter (Eddie)
Car keys (Eddie)
Wad of bills (Joey)
Matchbook with one match inside (Joey)
Bottle of cleaning fluid
Rifle (Tex)

Next Tuesday

Prison visitor's table
Wire screen
Chairs (2)
Purse (Bess)
Cigarettes (Mickey)
Bible (In purse)
Handmade wallet (Mickey)
Business Card (Mickey)

John's Ring

Sofa
Television cart
Television
Various apartment furnishings
TV dinner
Fork
Man's diamond ring
Phone
2 handbags (Amber & Stella)
Chewing gum (Amber)
Breath spray (Stella)
Spray can of mace (Amber)
Pencil (Stella)
Gold pen (Amber)
Pamphlet (Stella)
Book (Amber)
Paper clips (Stella)
Stapler (Amber)
YWCA Card (Stella)
Credit card (Amber)

Nights in Hohokus

Table
2 Chairs
Neon beer sign hanging U.C. (optional)
Bowl of pretzels
Various beer bottles, some empty, some full
Ashtray
Cigarettes (Manny)